IN THE WAY

(an elle keen suspense thriller —book 2)

ava strong

Ava Strong

Ava Strong is author of the REMI LAURENT mystery series, comprising six books (and counting); of the ILSE BECK mystery series, comprising seven books (and counting); of the STELLA FALL psychological suspense thriller series, comprising six books (and counting); of the DAKOTA STEELE FBI suspense thriller series, comprising six books (and counting); of the LILY DAWN suspense thriller series, comprising five books (and counting); the MEGAN YORK FBI suspense thriller series, comprising five books (and counting); the SOFIA BLAKE FBI suspense thriller series, comprising five books (and counting); the AMY RUSH FBI suspense thriller series, comprising five books (and counting); the ELLE KEEN FBI suspense thriller series, comprising five books (and counting); and the LEXI COLE suspense thriller series, comprising five books (and counting).

An avid reader and lifelong fan of the mystery and thriller genres, Ava loves to hear from you, so please feel free to visit www.avastrongauthor.com to learn more and stay in touch.

ISBN: 978-1-0943-9743-6

BOOKS BY AVA STRONG

ELLE KEEN FBI SUSPENSE THRILLER
IN THE DARK (Book #1)
IN THE WAY (Book #2)
IN THE EYES (Book #3)
IN THE NIGHT (Book #4)
IN THE SILENCE (Book #5)

AMY RUSH FBI SUSPENSE THRILLER
TWISTED TRUTH (Book #1)
TWISTED GAME (Book #2)
TWISTED SECRET (Book #3)
TWISTED FATE (Book #4)
TWISTED VOW (Book #5)

SOFIA BLAKE FBI SUSPSENSE THRILLER
NO ONE THERE (Book #1)
NO ONE LEFT (Book #2)
NO ONE HOME (Book #3)
NO ONE TO HELP (Book #4)
NO ONE LIKE THIS (Book #5)

MEGAN YORK FBI SUSPENSE THRILLER
YOU'LL BE SORRY (Book #1)
YOU'LL BE NEXT (Book #2)
YOU'LL BE MINE (Book #3)
YOU'LL BE FIRST (Book #4)
YOU'LL BE GONE (Book #5)

LILY DAWN FBI SUSPENSE THRILLER
STILL ALIVE (Book #1)
STILL HOPE (Book #2)
STILL AWAKE (Book #3)
STILL HERE (Book #4)
STILL MAD (Book #5)

REMI LAURENT FBI SUSPENSE THRILLER
THE DEATH CODE (Book #1)

THE MURDER CODE (Book #2)
THE MALICE CODE (Book #3)
THE VENGEANCE CODE (Book #4)
THE DECEPTION CODE (Book #5)
THE SEDUCTION CODE (Book #6)

ILSE BECK FBI SUSPENSE THRILLER
NOT LIKE US (Book #1)
NOT LIKE HE SEEMED (Book #2)
NOT LIKE YESTERDAY (Book #3)
NOT LIKE THIS (Book #4)
NOT LIKE SHE THOUGHT (Book #5)
NOT LIKE BEFORE (Book #6)
NOT LIKE NORMAL (Book #7)

STELLA FALL PSYCHOLOGICAL SUSPENSE THRILLER
HIS OTHER WIFE (Book #1)
HIS OTHER LIE (Book #2)
HIS OTHER SECRET (Book #3)
HIS OTHER MISTRESS (Book #4)
HIS OTHER LIFE (Book #5)
HIS OTHER TRUTH (Book #6)

DAKOTA STEELE FBI SUSPENSE THRILLER
WITHOUT MERCY (Book #1)
WITHOUT REMORSE (Book #2)
WITHOUT A PAST (Book #3)
WITHOUT PITY (Book #4)
WITHOUT HOPE (Book #5)

LEXI COLE SUSPENSE THRILLER
FEAR THE DARK (Book #1)
FEAR THE SILENCE (Book #2)
FEAR THE COLD (Book #3)
FEAR THE NIGHT (Book #4)
FEAR THE TRUTH (Book #5)

CHAPTER ONE

Laura Davis submerged her toes with a contented sigh, the warmth of the bathwater enveloping her like a liquid embrace. She leaned back against the curved edge of the porcelain tub, a dog-eared copy of "Hamlet" balanced in her hands. The steam from the water fogged up the edges of her glasses, and she pushed them back up the bridge of her nose with a soapy finger. Her eyes danced over Shakespeare's words, the familiar cadence of the Bard's language resonating deeply within her well-read soul. In these moments, amidst the soliloquies and tragedies, Laura found an escape from the methodical quietude of her librarian life.

"Frailty, thy name is woman!" she whispered to herself, her voice barely above the lapping water, relishing the bite of Hamlet's tongue as if tasting the acidity of a well-aged wine.

Then, without warning, the serenity shattered—a sharp creak pierced the air, jolting Laura's heart into her throat. She froze, a ripple disturbing the stillness of the bath as her hand twitched involuntarily, sending droplets of water cascading down the margins of the page. Silence reclaimed the room, thick and suffocating, as she strained her ears against the hollow echo that followed.

"Probably just the wind," she murmured, attempting to soothe the sudden spike of adrenaline. Yet the rational explanation fell flat in the silence that had now enveloped her cozy refuge. The creak had not been a usual groan of old wood or a benign contraction of timbers; it was deliberate, a foreboding herald.

Laura's pulse throbbed in her temples, each beat a drum of impending dread. The book lay forgotten in the water, its pages slowly bloating with moisture as her gaze fixed on the opaque glass of the bathroom door. What had once offered privacy now seemed a fragile barrier.

She was alone at home.

So often alone wherever she went... This thought gave her a shiver, and brought forth another jolt of fear.

With a cautious resolve that felt at odds with her trembling hands, Laura eased herself out of the porcelain embrace of the bathtub. Water dripped from her skin, pooling on the cold tile floor as she reached for the plush terrycloth robe hanging on the back of the door. She cinched it tightly around her waist, the fabric offering scant comfort against the shivers that weren't solely from the chill in the air.

Her bare feet whispered across the tiles as she approached the door, the sound magnified by the silence that seemed to press against her eardrums. The comforting scent of lavender bath salts was swiftly replaced by the musty anxiety that now filled her nostrils. She pressed an ear against the wood, hoping for some sign of normalcy, but the house remained silent—as if holding its breath.

Laura's fingers curled around the doorknob, cool metal against her palm serving as a grounding point amidst the swirling fear. She exhaled slowly, willing her heartbeat to quieten, and then turned the knob with a deliberate slowness that belied her inner urgency.

The door creaked open, a soft sigh in the stillness, revealing the darkened expanse of her living room. Moonlight fought a losing battle against the heavy drapes, casting only the faintest of silver lifelines across the floor. She stepped over the threshold, each movement purposefully light, her eyes straining to adjust to the void that her home had become.

For a moment, she allowed herself the hope that her fears were unfounded—that the noise had been nothing more than the idiosyncrasies of an aging house. But then, as her gaze swept across the familiar shapes of furniture, now rendered alien in the shadowed gloom, her eyes caught the source of her disquiet.

There, in the far corner where her favorite reading chair sat, was a figure. It was motionless, a darker shape against the dark backdrop, nearly invisible but for the wrongness of its presence. The solitary lamp that she'd left on cast its light in tremulous waves, throwing a dance of shadows upon the walls. And within that insidious ballet, the figure seemed to pulse with a menacing life of its own.

Laura's breath hitched, her body instinctively recoiling even as her mind raced to make sense of what she was seeing. This was no mere trick of the light, no fleeting fancy borne from the pages of Shakespeare. There was someone in her house—someone who did not belong, standing ominously still, as if waiting for the play to unfold.

Laura's mind, honed by years of absorbing complex narratives, snapped into a state of hyper-awareness as she confronted the real-life antagonist before her. Time seemed to stretch, each millisecond pregnant with decisions and potential movements. Her fingers tightened around the robe that was her only armor, the terrycloth offering a laughable semblance of protection.

"W-who are you?" she stammered. "Get out of my house!" She screamed.

The figure stood up straight, staring at her from under an upraised hood. Her breath caught in her throat, and the scream threatening to tear from her lungs remained dormant. She simply couldn't react, as if her body had gone suddenly numb.

Shock, fear paralysis, a small, rational portion of her mind whispered.

The figure advanced—a silent predator closing the distance between them. Without thought, Laura's body responded; muscle memory from self-defense classes at the local gym guiding her limbs. She lunged forward, attempting to catch the intruder off-balance with a well-aimed push aimed at the chest.

But the assailant was prepared, their own reflexes sharp and predatory. They moved with a grace that belied their sinister intent, sidestepping Laura's assault effortlessly. A cold hand, shockingly strong, clamped around her wrist, twisting it back with cruel precision.

Pain lanced up Laura's arm, drawing a gasp from her lips. Adrenaline surged, granting her a burst of frenzied strength. She kicked out, her foot connecting with the intruder's knee. There was a momentary give, an indication of human frailty, but it wasn't enough.

The struggle intensified, a macabre dance in the dimly lit room. Laura grasped for anything within reach, her fingers closing around the spine of a hardcover book from the coffee table. With a grunt, she swung it like a club, the edge of the tome striking the assailant's shoulder.

It should have halted them, perhaps even turned the tide in her favor, but the reaction was minimal, barely a flinch. The intruder seized the book from her grasp and tossed it aside with disdain. Their other hand shot out, finding her throat, squeezing with merciless intent.

Air became a precious commodity, slipping away with each passing second. Black splotches danced in her vision as Laura clawed at the iron-like grip. In a desperate bid for survival, she jabbed her elbow backward, hoping to connect with something—anything.

Her resolve was mighty, but the flesh was weak. The intruder's overpowering presence crushed her efforts with disheartening ease. As her struggle waned, the dark figure began to drag her, half-dragging, half-carrying her limp form back towards the bathroom.

Laura's consciousness flickered, her mind struggling to cling to the edges of reality. She could feel the cold tile of the bathroom floor against her feet, the eerie echo of their movement bouncing off the walls. Each step toward the tub, a dirge for her impending fate. Her robe, once a symbol of comfort, now felt like a shroud, trailing behind her as she was inexorably pulled closer to the water that awaited her.

Laura's senses dulled and blurred into obscurity, but the assailant's intent was coming into sharp, terrifying focus. Her limbs, unresponsive and heavy, seemed to float as if she were already submerged in the waters of her own demise. The cold rim of the bathtub pressed against the back of her knees, urging her downward with a lover's insistence.

As she was positioned with a disturbing reverence, Laura's mind, grasping at the tattered remains of Shakespearean verses, assembled the macabre tableau taking form. She was Ophelia, the tragic maiden of Elsinore, and this bathroom her riverbank. A mournful wail built within her chest, but surfaced only as a weak gurgle against the hand that had found its way once more to her throat.

The air was thick, laced with the scent of lavender bath salts and impending doom. It mingled with the weight of waterlogged paper as the intruder placed something onto her chest with an unsettling gentleness. Even in her compromised state, she could feel the texture of the page, swollen with moisture, contrasting against her skin.

Her eyes, though dimming, caught sight of ink-stained parchment, the immortal words of Hamlet distorted, replaced by a labyrinth of coded messages. In these cryptic glyphs lay a story untold, a perverse epilogue to her life's narrative written by an unseen author. Each symbol bore the weight of a final sentence, a judgment passed without trial.

The page clung to her like a death shroud, the script a requiem for the unwritten chapters of her existence. As the reality of her plight pierced the haze of her fading awareness, the room spun, and darkness threatened to claim her. Yet even in the encroaching void, Laura Davis, lover of literature and guardian of books, could not help but seek meaning in the twisted cipher resting upon her heart.

Laura's eyelids fluttered, a feeble defense as the shadowy visage of her assailant emerged from the gloom above. The contours of the killer's face were etched with an eerie calm that belied the violence of their actions. Eyes, dark and hollow like voids, stared down at her with an unreadable expression, imprints of a soul devoid of empathy. The cold draft in the room seemed to grow colder still, a spectral touch upon her damp skin.

Panic clawed at her throat, but her screams were mere whispers against the tightening grip. There was something profoundly unsettling in the way those eyes held her own—a chilling promise that her fate was sealed. This face, the harbinger of her demise, would be the final sight burned into her memory, a haunting specter that would follow her into the abyss.

The struggle within her ebbed, muscles yielding to the inevitable as her assailant maintained their silent watch. Laura's mind reeled, gasping for air and understanding, yet neither came. Her consciousness waned, flickering like the last glimmer of twilight before night's full embrace.

And then, the water rose to claim her.

As she drifted beneath the surface, the warmth of the bath became an ironic cradle to the cold reality of her end. Laura's limbs, once fighting with scholarly vigor, now floated with tragic grace around her—the final act of surrender. In these moments, the connection to Ophelia was painfully clear, an intimate resonance with the doomed heroine she had so often pondered over in the quiet of the library.

The tendrils of fear tightened around her heart as the realization crystallized; she was not just witnessing a macabre reflection of fiction, but living it. The ripples of water lapping against her cheeks sang a mournful lullaby, reminiscent of the flowers Ophelia had gathered before her watery descent. But there were no violets here—only the stark truth that her story would end in silence, unspoken and unheard, save for the coded enigma left behind.

The last echo of fear reverberated through her sinking consciousness—one final thought that encapsulated the horror of her plight, and then darkness fell.

CHAPTER TWO

Upon entering the briefing room, the atmosphere clung to Elle's skin—dense with expectation and seasoned with a tang of anxiety that only cases of high severity brought about. Screens lit up the dim space, casting angular shadows over the tense faces of her colleagues. They all looked to her as she slipped into an empty seat, her presence completing the circle of readiness.

"Thank you for joining us, Agent Keen," SAIC Harper began, his eyes briefly connecting with hers before flicking to the digital display on the wall. It was a crime scene photo, stark and cold in its detail. "This is Laura Davis," he said, indicating the woman in the image who lay still and pale.

"Her body was found this morning by a jogger who spotted a broken window and looked inside to investigate," he continued. A murmur rippled through the room, but Elle remained silent, her gaze locked onto the screen, absorbing every pixel of information.

"Initial forensics suggest she was posed post-mortem," Harper went on, flipping to another slide showing a peculiar arrangement of objects around the body. "A quick survey of her house found an entry point through the window. So, for now, the assumption is that Laura was killed in her home. But it's this that got our attention."

The image revealed a small tableau—a vintage typewriter, an inkwell, and a quill—arranged with meticulous care around the victim. It was as if someone had tried to frame the scene in a different time, a morbid diorama disconnected from the modern world.

"Any prints or DNA?" Elle interjected, her analytical mind already sifting through the chaos for strands of order.

"Clean," Harper confirmed with a nod. "Our killer knows what they're doing."

"Profiling?" Elle pressed further, her palms flat on the table, as if trying to press her own clarity into the unfolding narrative.

"Work in progress," Harper admitted, "but the staging suggests someone who's not just literate but literarily inclined. We're thinking this might not be an isolated incident."

"Copycat?" suggested one of the agents across the room.

"Or a serial in the making," Harper corrected grimly. "We need to move fast, people. Time's already against us. One other thing." Harper approached Elle, holding a piece of paper encased in an evidence baggie.

Elle's fingers brushed against the cold paper as it was handed to her, the texture betraying a faint ridged impression where ink had dried over hastily scrawled codes. Her gaze fastened onto the page, eyes flitting across the familiar lines of 'Hamlet', but they were marred, interrupted by an invasive script of numbers and symbols that clawed their way into Shakespeare's prose.

"Found tucked into Laura Davis' hand," Harper's voice cut through Elle's focus like a scalpel. "It's... unconventional."

"Unconventional" barely scratched the surface. Elle's brain hummed with activity, each synapse firing like a spark in dry tinder. The text before her wasn't just altered—it was a message in itself. The killer had replaced key words with an array of enigmatic characters, transforming the soliloquy into a cryptogram.

"Codes within literature..." Elle murmured under her breath, her pulse quickening at the challenge. Here lay a breadcrumb trail laid out by a twisted intellect—a game of cat and mouse penned by a murderer with a penchant for the dramatic.

"Keen?" Harper probed, noting her agent's sudden immersion into the puzzle.

"Give me some time with this," she replied, her voice steady despite the whirlwind of thoughts. Her instincts screamed that this wasn't the work of a one-off madman. This was methodical, planned, a performance by someone who relished the chase as much as the kill.

"Time is a luxury we might not have," Harper cautioned, his tone heavy with the weight of responsibility. "Already people!" he called out, turning to the room. "Let's get moving!" He clapped his hands together with the sound of a starter pistol.

Elle nodded, folding the page carefully and tucking it into her jacket pocket. She was already mentally cataloging her extensive knowledge of ciphers and encryption methods, her mind racing towards decryption even as she strode out of the room. The halls of the FBI Headquarters blurred past her, every step taking her closer to an adversary that seemed to dance just beyond reach, hidden behind a veil of literary subterfuge.

She hastily approached her work-station when a voice called out after her.

She turned sharply, jarred by the distraction, but her eyes leveled on Agent Tom Wright, her partner. Tom

stood there with a playful smirk on his face, his dark eyes twinkling with a mixture of amusement and curiosity.

"Hey there, Codebreaker," he said, his voice laced with an undercurrent of mischief which always seemed to reside there. "I couldn't help but notice that you've got that look in your eyes again."

"What look?"

"The one that tells me you're about to dive headfirst into a puzzle."

"Well, it is my job."

"Can't say hi to your own partner first, though?" he said, a teasing edge to his voice.

"Oh... were you in the room, too?"

He rolled his eyes and flashed a finger at her. It wasn't a very polite gesture, but she knew it was a joke.

A lot of Tom's behavior was meant to lighten the mood.

Tom Wright was every bit his father's son. His old man had a bit of a reputation in the FBI as a cowboy, but he'd solved cases, and his uncle had been on staff. Still, Tom lived in a long shadow... for the most part, Tom seemed to find this amusing. He was tough as nails when shit hit the fan, but while shooting the shit, everything seemed like a big joke to him.

He'd been at the FBI a few years longer than Elle. This was only her second year, and her first year as Tom's partner.

The two of them were different in their approach, but had proven an effective force, so far.

She allowed her gaze to linger momentarily on Tom's bulging muscles, visible straining against his tight suit. The suit was perfectly tailored to fit him and seemed to match the no-nonsense military cut he boasted. But his buzzed head and stoic posture clashed with his school-boy attitude. A combination of playful and dangerous, he kept her on her toes.

"So whadya think?" Tom said simply, crossing his impressive arms and studying her. She could see the thin lines of his cheekbones. He worked out more than most people slept, and managed to keep his body-fat percentage at an impressively low number, though she'd never mustered the courage to ask *what.*

"I think... it's similar to that other case," Elle said quietly. "Rebbeca Grey."

"Right," Tom said, snapping his fingers. "I forgot the victim's name. That was only a couple weeks ago, right?"

"Yeah. Was assigned to Carter and Yasmin."

"They're still working it?"

Elle shook her head. "They were moved to that witness protection detail. The case got shifted in the shuffle."

"Onto our desk?"

She looked back at the paper in the evidence bag. "Depends if they're connected or not."

"What makes you think they might be?"

"Rebecca's body was staged too, remember?"

"No."

She turned to her computer, pulling up the relevant case file, and opening the digital photos of the crime scene for the two of them to peruse.

As the gruesome images flickered on the screen, Elle pointed at the eerie similarities between the two crime scenes. "See here? Both victims were positioned in a deliberate manner, as if someone was trying to convey a message. The way their limbs were arranged, the placement of objects around them... it's too specific to be a coincidence."

Tom leaned in closer, his sharp eyes narrowing as he studied the photos. "You might be onto something, Keen. The level of precision and attention to detail is unsettling. It's like the killer is orchestrating a twisted work of art."

Elle nodded grimly, her mind racing with possibilities. "What if this isn't just about murder? What if there's a code hidden within these staged scenes?"

Her partner's eyebrows shot up in surprise. "Like some kind of cryptic message?"

She nodded again, her eyes shining with excitement. "Exactly! Think about it, Tom. The killer could be leaving behind clues, symbols, or even encrypted messages that serve as breadcrumbs for us to follow."

Tom scratched his head, his expression thoughtful. "But who would go through all that trouble just to taunt us? And why?"

Elle shrugged, her gaze never wavering from the screen. "That's what we need to find out. This killer is intelligent and meticulous. They want to challenge us, to prove that they are one step ahead. But we won't let them succeed."

Elle and Tom leaned in closer, their eyes fixated on the graphic images displayed on the computer screen. The crime scene photos were a chilling reminder of the gruesome work that awaited them. Elle's fingers danced across the keyboard, zooming in on specific details that caught her attention.

"Just like with Rebecca Grey, there's an eerie precision to the way the body is arranged," Elle said, her voice barely above a whisper. "Notice how the limbs are positioned symmetrically. It's almost artistic."

Tom nodded, his expression growing serious as he studied the images. "You're right, Elle. This isn't just a random act of violence. Someone took great care in staging these scenes."

Elle scrolled through more photos, her mind racing with possibilities. She had always been drawn to puzzles, but this case was different. It felt personal, as if someone was taunting her with each meticulously placed clue.

As they continued their analysis, Elle couldn't help but notice the striking similarities between Rebecca Grey and the current victim.

Both had dark hair. Both with pale skin. Both in their mid-twenties.

"Hey, look here," she said suddenly. "A piece of paper was recovered from Rebecca Grey's crime scene too." She clicked to photos of the evidence.

On the screen, she spotted a quill pen. And an old typewriter.

"Shit," Tom said. "They're the same. Same as Laura Davis' scene."

"And look," Elle said, her breath coming quickly. "Look!" she pointed adamantly.

And there, in the image, she found herself staring at a note. There was text in the image but too stained with blood to tell what it had once said. She frowned... but there, at the top of the page, she read the heading. *The Picture of Dorian...* "Gray," she finished where the page was too stained to read.

"Huh... Not more Shakespeare."

"No... No," she murmured. "But definitely a pattern."

"You know," Tom said, "I once heard Shakespeare was fake. That there was no one actually named Shakespeare."

"Yeah, well, I think that's stupid," she said absentmindedly, still staring at the photos. Sometimes, when distracted, she could be rude in ways she didn't intend to.

Tom raised an eyebrow. "Stupid, huh? You think it's stupid that there might be more to the story than what we've been told?"

Elle sighed, realizing she had been dismissive of Tom's comment. "No, I didn't mean it like that. It's just... Shakespeare is a widely accepted figure in history. To suggest he didn't exist seems far-fetched."

"Fair enough," Tom replied with a shrug. "But we can't deny the possibility that there's something hidden beneath the surface here."

Elle nodded, her mind still racing with the connections she was making. "I think we need to dig deeper into these victims' backgrounds. There must be something linking them beyond their appearances."

Tom leaned against the desk, crossing his arms over his chest. "Agreed. Whoever is behind this seems to have a specific type in mind. We need to find out why."

"Sorry," she added quickly. "You're not stupid. The comment was." She hesitated. This sounded blunt too now that she'd spoken it aloud. She sighed, wishing she'd learned social graces as much as code-breaking.

But Tom chuckled, taking her comment in stride. "Well, whether Shakespeare was real or not, I don't think this case has anything to do with him. But that note... 'The Picture of Dorian Gray'? That's a classic novel by Oscar Wilde."

"Exactly! It's not random. These staged crime scenes, the references to literature... it's all part of a twisted game the killer is playing."

"We need to find out who this killer is and why they're fixated on these literary references," Tom said, his voice determined.

Elle nodded, her mind already whirling with possibilities. "I'll start digging into any connections between the victims, focusing on their personal lives and interests. Maybe there's a link there that we've missed."

"Actually," Tom cut in, "the crime scene is on hold. We're supposed to get down there so they can release the techs."

"Alright. Crime scene first, then." Elle could feel her hackles rising, her excitement growing.

The two of them moved away from the desk, striding purposefully towards the exit.

CHAPTER THREE

Elle Keen's gaze lingered on the yellow tape fluttering in the breeze, a stark contrast to the manicured hedges and blooming hydrangeas that framed Laura Davis's colonial-style home. The neighborhood exuded a serenity wholly at odds with the horror it concealed behind polished oak doors. Pulling up in their unmarked FBI sedan, Elle could feel the weight of the scene ahead settling over her like a leaden cloak. Her hand tensed against the windowsill of the car as it often did when in a moving vehicle.

It didn't happen all the time, but occasionally, especially in high-pressure situations, her mind flitted back to her parents' collision.

The accident years ago that had forever sent her on the path of law enforcement. She shook her head, wincing, and loosening her grip on the sill, forcing her mind to focus, once again, on Laura' Davis' colonial-style home.

"Looks can be deceiving," she muttered under her breath, unbuckling her seatbelt with a decisive click.

"Isn't that the truth," Tom replied, his voice a steady baritone. He stepped out of the driver's side, straightening the lapels of his tailored blue suit, the pale poppy above his lapel catching the morning sun.

As they approached the entrance, Elle's analytical mind began its ritual dance of preparation, each step toward the house sharpening her focus. She breathed in deeply, taking in the scent of freshly cut grass mixed with the faintest hint of decay—a disturbing reminder that beneath this suburban idyll lay a gruesome tableau waiting for them.

Tom gave her a sidelong glance, the crease on his scarred face deepening. "Ready?"

"Always," Elle replied, her tone betraying none of the turmoil that churned within her. Her walnut hair stirred in the gentle wind, the solitary white streak at her bangs standing out defiantly. Elle never bothered to dye it; to her, it was a mark of authenticity in a world often shrouded in deception.

They crossed the threshold, stepping into the cool air of the foyer. Elle's keen eyes darted around, absorbing every detail. Not yet the chaos of the crime scene but instead the eerie quiet of a place violently disrupted and then abandoned to the silence of an unsolved mystery.

Elle's shadow fell across the threshold of the living room, a jagged line dividing order from chaos. The air was stale with an undercurrent of panic that lingered like a bad memory. She scanned the disarray—a cushion torn open with stuffing spilling onto the floor, a lamp tilted as if in mid-fall, frozen by time, and scuff marks darkening the carpet. The scene was a silent testament to a struggle that had turned fatal.

"Tom," she whispered, her eyes locking onto a smattering of glass shards near the fireplace. "Looks like the perp wasn't concerned with leaving traces behind."

"Or they wanted us to find them," Tom murmured, his gaze following hers.

Elle crouched, her fingers hovering above the debris but never touching. She studied the distribution of the fragments, noting how some were crushed into the carpet fibers while others lay unscathed, as though placed with intention. Methodical. Deliberate. Each clue was a piece of an elaborate puzzle, and Elle felt the familiar pull of unraveling its complexity.

"Let’s move on," she said, rising to her feet with a fluid grace that belied the weight of her thoughts. Together, they traversed the silent battlefield of a home once filled with life.

The transition was palpable as they approached the bathroom doorway. The silence deepened, pressing against Elle's eardrums with the weight of anticipation. It was here that Laura Davis's last act played out—an act not of her own making.

Inside, the stark white tiles gave off a sterile glow, but it was marred by splashes of red that drew the eye to the bathtub. A crimson-soaked cloth lay draped over the edge, its hue too vivid against the porcelain. The tub itself was a stage, meticulously arranged, the body posed.

"Someone went through a lot of trouble to set this up," Tom said, his voice hollow in the close confines.

The crime scene was girded with flowers lining the tub. An old sash dangled above the shower curtain, and willow branches lay along the floor near the window.

She stepped closer, careful not to disturb the tableau before her. Her mind raced, dissecting every choice the killer made—the positioning of the body, the selection of the scene, the implications of the drama they chose to enact. Ophelia had fallen out of a willow tree in the play. This was a stage upon which Elle knew she must perform flawlessly if she hoped to catch a killer who reveled in the macabre theatrics of murder.

Elle leaned in, her gaze sharpening as it caught the glint of dampened paper against the stillness of Laura Davis's skin. The page, unmistakably torn from a copy of 'Hamlet,' clung to the contours of her chest, each waterlogged fiber a testament to the killer's theatricality. But it was not the audacity of using Shakespeare as an instrument of death that seized Elle's attention—it was the deliberate obscuration of words, replaced by a sequence of letters and symbols that wove through the text like a serpent amongst branches. It matched the piece of paper that had been removed from Laura's hand by the evidence team.

This paper, though, was water-damaged, and had likely been left so they could see it before the crime scene was altered in any way.

"Tom," she murmured, not taking her eyes off the coded message. "This isn't just about literature. It's a challenge."

Through her peripheral vision, she saw Tom step closer, his own curiosity piqued. Elle could almost feel the gears turning in his mind as he peered over her shoulder at the cryptic alterations.

"Any idea what it means?" he asked quietly.

"Not yet," Elle replied. Her fingers itched for her phone, her body leaning unconsciously towards the promise of unraveling the enigma before her.

With a steadiness born of years threading through the webs of deceit and secrecy, Elle extracted her smartphone from her pocket. She angled the lens with precision, capturing the coded page in high resolution, ensuring that not a single mark was left out of focus. Each click of her camera was a silent vow to dissect the message, to strip away layers of subterfuge until truth lay bare.

"Got it," she said, more to herself than to Tom. The picture was clear, a perfect replica that would allow her to dive deep into analysis later—away from the chill of death that emanated from the porcelain grave before her. In that shrouded bathroom, amidst the quiet echoes of tragedy, Elle's mind was already alight with theories, patterns beginning to form in the chaos of her thoughts. Every encrypted word was a piece of the puzzle, beckoning her to delve into the psyche of a murderer who wielded prose as a weapon.

"Let's make sure we get this back to the lab, intact," she instructed, sliding her phone back into her pocket with newfound resolve. The image of the page, now seared into her memory, promised a battle of wits she was more than ready to accept.

Elle stepped back from the bathroom threshold, her gaze sweeping across the living room once more. Chaos had descended upon it, but it was a calculated sort of disarray. Bookshelves that once bore the weight of literature and knickknacks were now upended, their contents strewn yet strangely orderly. A circle of disruption radiated outward from the epicenter of struggle, as if each overturned chair and shattered vase had been deliberately placed.

"Look at this," she called out softly, her voice steady despite the surge of adrenaline.

Tom approached, his eyes scanning the area Elle gestured toward. "What is it?"

"Precision," she replied, kneeling beside a toppled stack of books. Her fingers traced the spines, noting the absence of dust—a sign of frequent handling. "Our killer doesn't do random. This mess... it's meticulous. They wanted us to see the struggle, but it's a controlled scene."

"Choreographed," Tom added, his gut instincts aligning with her observations.

"Exactly." Elle stood, her eyes never ceasing in their detailed sweep. "And there's a profound understanding of literature here. Not just any books are scattered—it's the classics, the heavy hitters of literary canon."

"Following a theme..." Tom mused, catching on to Elle's line of thought.

"Potentially," Elle agreed, the cogs in her mind whirring faster. "The coded 'Hamlet' page on Laura's chest wasn't chosen by happenstance. It's a message, a calling card. Our killer might be using literature not just as inspiration but as a blueprint for murder."

"Like they're recreating scenes from the books?" Tom's voice was laced with a mix of disbelief and dawning comprehension.

"Perhaps," she said, her tone contemplative. "Or maybe it's more symbolic. The choice of 'Hamlet'—a tale of revenge, madness, and tragedy—it could be significant."

"Could be their signature, too," Tom surmised, running a hand over his crew-cut. "Using the stories to leave their mark, to challenge us..."

"Or to taunt us." Elle's eyes hardened at the thought. "If we assume this theory holds water, our killer isn't just well-read; they're intellectual, arrogant even. They believe they can outsmart us by weaving their crimes into the fabric of literary history."

"Then let's prove them wrong," Tom said, the muscle in his jaw clenching with determination.

"Agreed." Elle's gaze lingered on the chaos one last time before she turned to Tom with a resolute expression. "We'll need to dive deep into these texts, look for patterns or upcoming 'anniversaries' in literary works. Anything that might hint at their next move."

Tom nodded, his dark eyes reflecting the same fire that burned within her. "We'll catch this literate lunatic," he affirmed. "Let's get to work."

Elle glanced around the living room once more, but then turned, frowning and moving back to the bathroom.

She approached the body.

This was the focal point of the play, where the audience's eyes were meant to linger.

If the killer was playing a game, then would he have staged it here?

Elle hunched closer, her breath a controlled whisper against the page sprawled on Laura's unmoving chest. The room's stillness seemed to lean in with her, as if the very air waited for her to unearth its secrets. Her fingers hovered, careful not to disturb the crime scene more than necessary.

"Something's not right," she muttered, brows knitting together over keen eyes that swept across the text. She followed the coded words, her mind deftly cataloging every aberration from Shakespeare's original script. Then, there it was—a subtle inconsistency, a faint patterning that didn't belong to the aged paper.

"Tom, get the alternate light source," Elle said without looking up, her voice a mix of excitement and command.

"Found something?" Tom approached, his heavy steps reverberating softly in the tense atmosphere.

"Maybe." Elle angled her head, allowing the overhead light to catch the page just so. "There." A ghost of a smile touched her lips as she pointed to a barely-there symbol, a watermark that could only be seen when the page was held at a precise angle against the light.

"Is that...?" Tom leaned in, squinting at the mark.

"Could be a custom watermark. Not something you'd find on your run-of-the-mill book paper," Elle replied, her mind already racing through the implications. This wasn't the work of a commonplace killer; this was someone who left their signature hidden in plain sight.

"Careful now," she continued, straightening up as Tom retrieved a pair of tweezers and evidence bags from his kit. "We need to preserve every fiber on this page. It might tell us who we're dealing with."

"Got it." Tom's movements were methodical, honed by years of experience, as he slipped the page into a clear bag, sealing it with practiced ease.

"Good. Let's get this to the lab ASAP. I want to know where that watermark came from," Elle said, her pulse quickening with the prospect of a new lead. "And let's hope our literate friend made a mistake leaving us this clue."

"Whoever they are, they haven't met Elle Keen yet," Tom added with a half-grin, meeting her gaze with unwavering confidence.

"Let's keep it that way," Elle replied, the streak of white in her hair catching the light as she turned back to the scene, her mind already dissecting the next move in this deadly game of intellects.

Stepping back across the threshold of Laura's home, Elle felt the air change from the stifling stillness of a crime scene to the open breath of the outside world. Her boots clicked against the concrete path, each step resonating with purpose and newfound energy. The suburban street lay quiet, its tranquility now a stark contrast to the macabre tableau she left behind.

Elle glanced back at the house, her eyes narrowing as if to etch every detail into her recollection—the angle of the blinds, the color of the door, the way the yellow police tape carved out the perimeter of a predator's playground.

"Keen?" Tom's voice broke through her focus, tinged with concern and anticipation.

She thought of the coded message, the watermark. These were signatures not just of a crime, but of a challenge—a puzzle meticulously crafted by someone who reveled in the cryptic and the theatrical. It was an invitation to dance on a razor's edge, and Elle was poised to accept.

Her heart thrummed with adrenaline, not from fear, but from the thrill of the chase. This was where she thrived, in the realm of riddles and revelations. She reached for the door handle of their unmarked vehicle.

"Chinese for lunch?" Tom suggested his attempt at normalcy a stark juxtaposition to the gravity of their task. "You need to eat."

"Later," she replied curtly, hunger paling in comparison to the craving for answers. With a deft motion, she slid into the passenger seat, her gaze fixed on the horizon.

"Alright, Elle," Tom conceded, starting the engine. "We play this your way."

As the car pulled away from the curb, Elle didn't look back. There was no room for hesitation, not when lives hung in the balance. In her mind, the game had already begun—a complex cat-and-mouse pursuit that would demand all her acumen.

A literate killer was on the loose, cloaked in Shakespearean guise, and Elle Keen was the codebreaker in a high-stakes thriller written in blood and ciphers. The hunt was on, and she was ready.

CHAPTER FOUR

The fluorescent lights buzzed overhead, casting a sterile glow on the stainless steel surfaces of the FBI forensics lab. The air was thick with concentration, every expert in their element amidst the meticulous dissection of evidence. Elle Keen pushed through the double doors with purpose, her hair swishing against the stark white coat she'd donned at the entrance.

"Keen, glad you could join us," greeted the lead technician without looking up from his microscope.

Dr. Spakes was distracted by his work, but Elle knew there were few better. Spakes was wearing a vibrant Hawaiian shirt, and his wild hair jutted out from under a flat cap. She approached his station, her eyes scanning the array of equipment and samples that covered the table.

"What do we have, Spakes?" she asked, her voice steady and focused.

Spakes glanced up from his microscope, a mischievous twinkle in his kind eyes. "Ah, Agent Keen," he said with a heavy German accent. "I've been expecting you. Look at this." He gestured toward a slide under the lens, magnifying it before her eyes.

Elle peered through the microscope, her heart quickening as she observed the intricate pattern etched on the glass slide. It was a series of delicate lines and curves, forming a cryptic design that seemed to dance before her eyes.

"It's mesmerizing," Elle murmured.

"Yes, indeed," Spakes replied with a proud grin.

"What is it?"

"My lunch," Spakes said with a chuckle. And then he reached out, plucking a small piece of candy off the viewing tray and popping it into his mouth.

Elle blinked in surprise as Tom also entered the room behind them.

Tom Wright followed closely behind Elle, his towering frame filling the doorway. His tailored blue suit, adorned with a pale poppy lapel pin, seemed almost ceremonial against the backdrop of lab coats and latex gloves. He scanned the room with a practiced eye, the scar on his face a stark reminder of the unpredictability inherent in their line of work.

Elle nodded curtly at Spakes and moved towards the central table where Laura Davis's crime scene artifacts lay spread out like a grim jigsaw puzzle. Her gaze swept across the array, each piece a silent witness waiting to divulge its secrets. She leaned closer, her mind already sifting through possibilities, patterns, meanings—her craving for Chinese food momentarily forgotten in the face of the enigma before her.

"Let's get started," she said, her voice steady, betraying no hint of the past that haunted her or the memories that fueled her relentless drive. In the reflection of the polished tabletop, Tom's dark eyes met Elle's, an unspoken agreement passing between them. They were here to unravel a mystery, and time was of the essence.

Elle rolled up her sleeves, the fabric tightening around her forearms as she settled into the sterile realm of the forensic lab. The hum of precision equipment played a steady rhythm as she gravitated toward a microscope stationed amidst a landscape of evidence markers and digital displays. Her fingers traced the ridges of a blood spatter pattern printed on a glossy photograph before she refocused her attention on the task at hand.

"Let's magnify these ink-blots," she suggested, the words crisp, her inherent command drawing an immediate response from the technician beside her. Adjusting the microscope's settings, she peered through the eyepiece with an intensity that made her surroundings fade into obscurity.

Spakes muttered to himself as he finagled the machines with the expertise of a longtime lover.

The black splodges bloomed under the scrutiny of high magnification, revealing their true nature. Elle's breath caught as the intricate feathering edges and pooling gradients of the ink spoke volumes to her analytical mind. She straightened, turning to the technician. "Take a look."

"Please," Tom added.

Spakes leaned in, peering at the image in question. "Ah," he said.

"Yes?"

"This is vintage fountain pen ink," he declared confidently, looking up with an eagerness, like a golden retriever expecting praise.

"You're sure?" Elle said.

He looked offended. "It's not something you find in your everyday ballpoint pen from a convenience store. Yes. I'm sure."

Tom loomed nearby, his presence a silent bulwark.

"An eccentric choice for our killer," Elle mused aloud, her eyes not leaving the enlarged image of the ink-blots. "Someone who appreciates the permanence of the past, perhaps." The idea seemed to resonate with her, a kindred understanding of the reverence one might hold for history—with its unchanging script and indelible marks—mirroring her own quest for immutable truths in a profession riddled with uncertainties.

Elle leaned back, her gaze fixed on the air above the microscope as though projecting her thoughts onto an invisible screen only she could see. The lab buzzed around her, a symphony of scientific pursuit, but in her mind, the melody was singular and clear: the distinctiveness of the fountain pen.

"Antiquated methods for modern madness," she murmured, almost to herself. Tom glanced over, catching the words that seemed to dance on the edge of a revelation. "What's that?" he asked.

"Think about it," Elle replied, her voice gaining traction as her ideas coalesced. "Our killer didn't choose a fountain pen by accident. It's personal, deliberate. It suggests a longing for an era long gone—or perhaps a disdain for the impersonal nature of today's world."

Tom nodded, absorbing her deduction. His eyes reflected a spark of admiration; Elle's ability to find meaning in minutiae never failed to impress him.

"Old or nostalgic..." Elle continued, tapping a finger against her lips. "Someone who cherishes the past enough to use it as their medium." She stood, pushing the chair away with a purposeful movement.

"Let's see if they cherish their secrets just as much." Elle's hand was steady as she reached for the coded message once again. She regarded the complex script with the same intensity she reserved for her favorite spicy Szechuan noodles—another puzzle to unravel, another layer of flavors to dissect.

As her eyes traveled over the cryptic symbols, her pulse quickened. Codes were her comfort, her element.

"Here we go," she whispered, her fingers dancing across the tablet as she input variables, testing hypotheses in rapid succession. With each passing moment, the coded message began to yield under the pressure of her relentless intellect, like a lock tumbling open under the right combination.

The room faded, the clamor of the lab reduced to a mere whisper against the roaring tide of her concentration. Elle Keen was in her domain, deciphering a language spoken by precious few—a language of truth that promised to lead her one step closer to the mind behind the ink-blots that held Laura Davis's final story.

Elle leaned in closer, her eyes narrowing as she scrutinized the structured style and format of the coded message sprawled across the screen. The characters seemed to waltz in a deliberate sequence, each step meticulously choreographed. A pattern began to emerge from the chaos, whispering secrets only Elle's trained eye could discern.

"Tom, look at this," she said, her voice steady with a controlled excitement. "The repetition here and here,"—her finger tapped against the tablet—"it's not random. It's too consistent."

Tom peered over her shoulder, his brow furrowed beneath the stark line of his crew-cut. His gaze followed her pointing finger, trying to catch a glimpse of the world through Elle's analytical lens.

"Could be a recurring sequence," Elle continued, her thoughts spilling out as she spoke. "If we can crack the pattern, it might just spell out our motive."

"Patterns, huh?" Tom grunted, his gut instincts kicking in. "Let's run it through the algorithms, see what comes up."

Elle nodded, her mind already racing ahead. She beckoned Gerald T. Spakes over, who had been tinkering with the equipment on the other side of the lab. His wild silver curls bobbed as he approached, a stark contrast to Tom's disciplined appearance.

"Got something for me to do, Miss Keen?" Gerald asked, his thick German accent coating his words with an affable warmth.

"Absolutely, Gerald," Elle replied, motioning towards the tablet. "We need to apply the advanced decryption algorithms on these sequences. Think you can set that up?"

"Of course!" Gerald exclaimed, his kind eyes twinkling behind round glasses. He set to work immediately, his fingers flying over the keyboard with surprising agility for a man adorned in such a vibrant Hawaiian shirt.

As Gerald configured the software, Elle's mental gears turned with precision. She watched the screen intently, her every synapse firing in anticipation. The algorithm chewed through the code like a key grinding into a stubborn lock.

"Here it comes," Gerald announced, leaning back to allow Elle and Tom a better view. Lines of potential decryptions streamed down the display, a waterfall of data filtered through the sieve of their collective expertise.

"Wait, stop there!" Elle commanded suddenly, pointing to a segment of the output. "That looks like it could be English—reverse the cipher."

"Reversing now," Gerald complied, his amiable demeanor unshaken by the urgency in her tone.

A string of coherent text materialized on the screen, snatching Elle's breath away. Her heart skipped a beat as she read the decrypted section, her mind piecing together the implications.

"Wait... wait, mind if I?"

Spakes nodded, stepping aside.

Elle's fingers moved deftly, as if playing a complex piece on a piano, tapping and swiping through databases while the algorithm continued to unravel the intricate web of code. The lab was a cacophony of electronic hums and clicks, punctuated by the low murmur of analysts discussing findings. Tom stood beside her, their shoulders almost touching in solidarity, his eyes scanning every new line of text that appeared on the screen.

Elle's mind, sharp as a scalpel, refused to succumb to fatigue. It was as though every unsolved riddle from her past had led to this moment, to this sequence of symbols that held the key to Laura Davis's killer.

"Anything?" Tom asked, his voice a grounding force amidst the storm of data.

"Close," Elle murmured, her focus unwavering. "Very close."

And then she paused. The page in question displayed a line of text. Most of the words didn't match. But in the middle, six did.

They simply read, *The heart of a bygone era...*

She stared at the line.

"It... it makes no sense," Tom said, staring over her shoulder.

But she frowned at the line. Then, putting it in quotes, she entered a search on the internet.

And waited.

Very few pages showed up. The search engine recommended portions of the phrase as the result, but then, at the bottom of the screen, she saw it.

"Wait... who's this?"

She frowned. *Mike Richards,* Tales From the Treatise.

"A book?" Tom said.

"Yeah. Looks like this is a line from that book."

"No reviews," Tom pointed out.

Elle scrolled down to the sales ranking. No sales either. This was a vanity book--something no one had read, nor would likely read.

So her attention shifted to the Author section.

"Mike Richards," she murmured.

The glow from the monitor illuminated their faces as they leaned in, the search results painting a picture of Mike Richards. He wasn't just a name; he was flesh and blood, a local literature professor with a penchant for Shakespearean plays and a reputation for cracking Elizabethan codes.

"An expert in decoding Shakespeare..." Elle mused out loud, the gears in her head already turning. "That's not your everyday hobby."

"Especially when tied to a murder case with ciphers," Tom added, the implication hanging between them like a charged particle. "This is more than a coincidence."

"Much more," Elle agreed. "Let's see what Professor Richards knows about our play," Elle said, her tone resolute. They'd found a crack in the case wide enough to peer through, and she was ready to shine a light on the truth hidden behind it.

Elle snapped the computer lid shut, the click echoing a sense of finality in the sterile room. With every second ticking by, Laura Davis's murderer wove a tighter web of riddles and taunts. But now, they had a name that cut through the ambiguity like the beam of a lighthouse slicing through fog.

"Tom, we need to move, now!" Elle's voice was a whip-crack in the silence of the forensics lab, jolting her partner into action.

Tom nodded, reading the urgency in her eyes. They gathered their notes and equipment with swift, practiced movements. Elle could feel the hum of adrenaline beneath her skin, a familiar sensation that sharpened her focus rather than muddling it.

She strode out of the lab, her mind already racing ahead to the confrontation with Mike Richards. The fluorescent lights of the FBI headquarters flickered overhead, casting stark shadows on the walls. Yet, in her vision, they only served to outline the path forward.

Why had a line from his book been in the code?

Other words... many others... hadn't responded to the algorithmic input. But it wasn't a coincidence. She couldn't see how it could possibly be an accident.

Mike Richards was involved.

The killer? Perhaps.

"Elle, wait up!" Tom called after her, his footsteps quickening to match her brisk pace.

"Every minute we waste is a minute he has to cover his tracks," she tossed over her shoulder, not breaking stride.

They burst through the exit doors and into the parking lot, where the late afternoon sun cast a golden glow over everything. Elle shielded her eyes for a moment, then darted towards their unmarked car, her hand already reaching for the door handle.

"Where to?" Tom asked as he slid into the driver's seat.

"Mike Richards' office at the university," Elle said, strapping herself in. "If he's as passionate about Shakespeare as his profile suggests, maybe he can interpret more than just plays."

The engine roared to life, and Tom navigated the vehicle smoothly onto the road. As buildings and trees blurred past the window, Elle felt the weight of expectation in her chest. This was it—the chase, the hunt for truth. And she was ready to confront whatever secrets Professor Richards held, ready to decipher the role he played in this dark and twisted drama.

"Let's hope he's willing to talk," Tom murmured, glancing at Elle.

"He will," she replied with a steely determination. "He doesn't have a choice."

CHAPTER FIVE

Elle Keen's shadow stretched long over the cobblestone path as she and Tom Wright made their approach, the gothic spires of the university reaching into the sky like skeletal fingers. The ancient bricks and mortar of the institution stood stoic against time, a perfect sanctuary for someone who found solace in the enduring words of Shakespeare and his contemporaries.

"Feels like we stepped onto the pages of a Brontë novel," Elle muttered, her voice barely a whisper against the grandeur of the architecture around them.

"Or into one of Poe's stories," Tom added, his eyes scanning the scene with a detective's precision. His imposing frame seemed to belong to another era, akin to the guardians chiseled from stone that watched over the hallowed halls. The poppy stitched above his lapel caught a glint of sunlight as they moved, a small touch of color on his otherwise serious attire.

The university exuded a sense of timeless knowledge, an atmospheric pressure that weighed down on Elle like a challenge. It was here, among these vaulted ceilings and whispered secrets, that their suspect wove narratives out of the lives he touched—both literary and literal.

She felt it, the echo of her parents' voices, encouraging her to look closer, to decipher the hidden messages in plain sight. But amidst the legacy of academia, Elle also sensed the isolation she often felt; a mind set apart by its own design.

"Let's hope Richards is more transparent than these cloistered walls," Elle said, her eyes narrowing slightly as they approached the Literature Department, where their suspect held court among the musty tomes of his profession.

"Transparency isn't exactly common in our line of work," Tom replied, the hint of a smile softening his rugged features.

"Neither are clear-cut answers," Elle countered, her hand resting momentarily on the pistol concealed beneath her jacket, "but I still prefer them over chaos."

Their footsteps echoed against the gothic arches, a drumbeat to the mystery that lay ahead. As they neared the door to Mike Richards' office, the air seemed to thicken with the anticipation of confrontation. Elle's mind raced through possible scenarios, each one a puzzle she was determined to solve. She was ready to peel back the layers of deceit, to chase down the truth no matter how deeply it was buried within the ivied walls of this scholarly haven.

As they approached the professor's door, hastening down the hall, Elle Keen maneuvered through the throngs of students with a practiced ease, Tom a steady presence at her side. The youthful energy of the campus buzzed around them—a stark contrast to the solemnity of their purpose.

The ornate doorway to Mike Richards' office was slightly ajar, wedged open by a leather-bound volume of Chaucer's works. Elle noted the spine worn from frequent use. Pushing the door further, they stepped into an enclave that felt more like a sanctuary dedicated to the written word than a mere workplace. Walls lined with towering bookshelves reached toward the high ceiling, each shelf densely populated with books whose rich leathers and faded spines spoke of centuries past. The scent of old paper and ink wafted through the air, mingling with a hint of sandalwood—likely from the incense perched on a small, carved table near the window.

"Professor Richards?" Elle called out, her voice firm yet respectful of the scholarly haven they'd entered.

A rustle from behind a stack of books was followed by the appearance of a man whose gaze darted from the badge in Elle's hand to their steely eyes. His hair was a tangle of graying curls, and his glasses sat askew on his nose as if they were an afterthought. There was an air of distracted intelligence about him, the kind that often shrouded those who lived more in the realm of ideas than reality.

"Can I help you?" His voice was tinged with an edge of skepticism that seemed to rise from the depths of his throat, a wary note that didn't escape Elle's attention.

"Professor Mike Richards, I presume?" Elle said, her own skepticism mirroring his. "I'm Agent Keen, and this is Agent Wright. We have a few questions for you."

Richards' eyes narrowed almost imperceptibly, a silent alarm bell that resonated with Elle's intuition. She observed the slight tightening of his shoulders, the flutter of his fingers as they brushed against the desk—a symphony of subtle tells that she read as clearly as the cryptography puzzles of her youth.

"Questions?" Richards echoed, the wariness now evident in his tone. "About what, may I ask?"

"Let's just say it pertains to your expertise," Elle replied, not missing the brief flicker of something like apprehension crossing his face. "And that it's very important you answer them honestly."

"Of course," he said, though his voice betrayed the unease that lay beneath the surface. "Honesty is paramount in academia, after all."

Elle leaned forward, her hands on the carved oak desk that separated her from Richards. "Professor, you're known for your work on ciphers in Elizabethan texts. Specifically, those embedded within Shakespeare's plays. Fascinating topic."

Richards nodded, a touch too eagerly, his hands clasping and unclasping. "Yes, it's a passion of mine. The Bard often played with hidden meanings."

"Did Laura Davis share this passion? Was she involved in any of your work?" Elle's voice was steady, but her gaze was piercing – searching.

"Involved? No, not directly." The professor's forehead creased as he frowned. "She attended a few of my lectures, though. A bright young woman, very inquisitive."

He hadn't denied knowing her. Elle blinked in surprise. She hadn't even known Laura had been auditing the classes. A lucky break? Or were they right about Mike's involvement.

He seemed casual about it, cavalier even, but this attitude wouldn't last.

"And where were you the night she was murdered?" Her question hung in the air like a weight, pressing down on the silence that grew between them.

He stared at her, eyes bugging. "M-murdered?" he stammered.

Elle's heart quickened at his reaction. The professor's mask of calm intellectualism had slipped, revealing a flicker of fear in his eyes. She watched as he tried to regain his composure, his fingers nervously tracing the edge of the desk.

Elle mentally noted the flicker of panic that crossed Richards' face, the tremor in his voice. It was a telling reaction, one that only confirmed her suspicions. She had struck a nerve.

"Yes, Professor Richards," she said, her voice cutting through the tension. "Laura Davis was found dead last night, and we believe you may have some information that could help us solve this case."

"L-last night? You're not serious."

Richards swallowed hard, his adam's apple bobbing in his throat. Beads of sweat formed on his brow as he stammered out a response. "I... I didn't know her well. Just a student who attended my lectures occasionally."

Elle studied him closely, searching for any signs of deception. She knew that the truth was often buried beneath layers of deceit, and it was her job to uncover it.

"Are you sure about that, Professor?" Tom interjected, his voice low and probing. "We have reason to believe that Laura Davis had a connection to your research on ciphers."

Richards shifted uncomfortably in his chair, avoiding their gaze. "I... I might have shared some information with her," he finally admitted, his voice barely audible. "But only in class... then, after. She spoke to me. Briefly."

"You remember this interaction with a student? How come?"

"She was memorable... I have a memory for names."

Elle's mind raced, connecting the dots in her head. Laura's interest in ciphers, her attendance at Richards' lectures—that was no mere coincidence. There was something more at play here, something hidden within the words and codes they were unraveling.

"What did you share with her?" Elle asked, her voice steady but insistent.

The professor hesitated before answering, seemingly torn between telling the truth. "I don't remember," he said at last. He shrugged. "Besides, I couldn't have harmed her. You said she was hurt last night, yes?"

"Killed," Tom replied.

"Where were you," Elle pushed.

"Here," Richards stammered, "working late on a manuscript. Alone."

"Alone," Elle echoed. A single word that seemed to echo off the walls lined with leather-bound volumes of literary classics.

"Agent Keen, I assure you—"

"Professor Richards," Elle cut him off, her eyes never leaving his face. "When a student of literature is found dead, inscribed with quotes from Hamlet, and you, an expert on Shakespearean codes are involved, it's more than coincidental. Don't you agree?"

He swallowed hard, his Adam's apple bobbing visibly. "Coincidental, yes. But implicating? Surely, you don't believe—"

"Belief isn't part of the equation," Elle said coolly. "Evidence is. And we're gathering it."

Richards' fingers twitched again, brushing against a dog-eared copy of 'Macbeth'. His gaze flitted toward the window, then back to Elle. Sweat beaded at his temple, despite the chill that lingered in the book-heavy air.

"Look, I didn't know her well. Why would I hurt her?" His voice had risen, a note of desperation threading through the words.

"Sometimes the narrative we write for ourselves diverges from reality, Professor," Elle observed, her mind sifting through the verbal and non-verbal cues he was giving off. "The truth has a way of surfacing, even from the most cryptic depths."

"Truth..." Richards murmured, suddenly looking smaller, dwarfed by the towering shelves of knowledge around him. "A double-edged sword, isn't it, Agent Keen?"

"Sharper than any dagger in your plays," Elle replied, watching him closely, aware that beneath his scholarly façade, there was something frayed, something unraveling. And she was determined to pull at the thread.

Professor Richards' eyes darted once more to the window, the muscles in his jaw clenching visibly. Elle watched the subtle shift in his posture, a coiled readiness that had nothing to do with academic debate. His hand moved toward the edge of the desk, fingers drumming an erratic rhythm.

"Agent Keen, I think this interview has concluded," Richards said abruptly, rising from his chair with a swiftness that belied his scholarly demeanor.

"Sit down, Professor," Tom's voice was a calm command, but Richards seemed not to hear it.

Elle's mind raced, detecting the escalation before it erupted into action. "We're not done here, Professor—"

But Richards was already moving, his exit neither graceful nor apologetic, as he barreled past them, papers scattering from the impact. Elle's instinct kicked in hard and fast, her codebreaker's mind calculating the odds of what he was trying to hide.

"Stop him!" Tom shouted, already giving chase.

Elle followed suit, her training taking over as they burst out of the office into the corridor. Students turned at the commotion, their faces registering shock and curiosity, books clutched to their chests as they stepped aside.

"Out of the way!" Tom bellowed, his FBI badge now on full display.

The chase unfurled like a scene from one of Richards' beloved tragedies. They sprinted past glass-encased bulletin boards announcing poetry readings and seminars, the echo of their footsteps mingling with the distant hum of intellectual discourse.

Through the Literature Department's double doors, Richards wove with surprising agility, his flight fueled by a palpable desperation. Elle's lungs burned, the sharp staccato of her breaths cutting through the musty silence of the university library they now threaded.

"Excuse me! Move!" Elle called out, sidestepping a startled student who nearly dropped a stack of books. The scent of old paper and leather-bound knowledge was a stark contrast to the adrenaline surging through her veins.

Richards dashed between aisles, sending a cascade of pages fluttering to the ground. They were close enough to hear his labored breathing, a testament to the fear driving him forward.

"Richards, stop!" Elle's authoritative voice sliced through the quietude, earning her the wide-eyed stares of students nestled in their studies.

But the professor was relentless, pushing through the emergency exit into the sunlight that flooded the quad. Their pursuit continued, a kinetic blur against the backdrop of collegiate gothic architecture.

Elle's focus narrowed, every footfall a determined beat, her keen eyes locked on the fleeing figure.

Tom's boots echoed through the cavernous space of the old auditorium, their pursuit of Richards reaching a crescendo. The antique sconces that lined the walls flickered, casting erratic shadows that danced with each of their movements. Dust motes swirled in the spotlight shafts that broke through the aging curtains, as if highlighting the stage for this unforeseen climax.

"Enough, Richards!" Tom's voice was a commanding boom that seemed to shake the rafters. He had him cornered now, the professor's back against the faded grandeur of velvet drapes.

Richards' eyes darted frantically, seeking an escape where there was none. With a desperate and clumsy vigor, he lunged at Tom, his arms flailing like broken quills of a pen that had written too many tragedies. But Tom was ready, sidestepping and catching one of the flailing arms, twisting it behind Richards in a fluid motion that belied his muscular frame.

"Stop resisting," Tom growled, securing Richards with a practiced restraint hold. Their bodies grappled, a tangle of limbs and strained breaths that filled the silent auditorium with the sounds of struggle.

Elle rushed in mere moments later, her own breath coming in sharp bursts from the chase. Her eyes swiftly took in the scene: Tom, standing firm as an immovable force, and Richards, now subdued, his body slumping in defeat. She approached cautiously, her mind racing with the same intensity as her pulse.

"Mike Richards, you are under arrest," Tom stated flatly as he clicked the handcuffs around the suspect's wrists.

Elle knelt in front of Richards, peering into his eyes—those windows that could sometimes reveal the truths hidden deep within a person. His gaze met hers, and she saw it then, the flicker not of malice but of panic that shimmered beneath the surface. His pupils were dilated, his forehead beaded with perspiration despite the coolness of the auditorium.

"Talk to me, Richards. What are you so afraid of?" Elle's voice softened, her innate ability to read people surfacing amidst the chaos. There was something off about this man, something that didn't quite fit the profile of a cold-blooded killer.

Richards' lips quivered, his breath hitching as he tried to form words, but nothing came out save for the ragged inhale and exhale of fear. Elle sensed it then, an intuition honed by years of decrypting the most intricate puzzles—the truth that Richards might not be their murderer, that his actions weren't those of guilt over a crime but rather a profound fear of something else entirely.

"Elle," Tom said, breaking into her thoughts, "we should get him back to the station."

She nodded, standing up and taking one last look at Richards. This man was a book with a cipher they hadn't cracked yet, and Elle couldn't shake the feeling that the real story lay in the spaces between his stammered breaths and wild, fearful eyes.

Elle's fingers curled into fists at her sides, the adrenaline from the chase still humming through her veins as they escorted Richards down the worn steps of the auditorium. Her eyes never left the man, his hands now cuffed behind him, his shoulders slumped in defeat. Tom's hand was firm on Richards' elbow, guiding him with an assertive gentleness that belied the intensity of moments ago.

The cacophony of the campus faded into a distant murmur as Elle's mind whirred, piecing together the fragments of behavior and misplaced fear she'd witnessed. Richards was a puzzle, but not the one she had hoped to solve. His nervous energy didn't carry the weight of guilt for the crime they were investigating; it was something else, something personal and perhaps just as desperate.

"Keen, you alright?" Tom's voice pierced her concentration, his gaze flicking to her as they passed beneath the archway leading out of the building.

Elle nodded, her resolve hardening. "Yeah," she replied, her tone even, betraying none of the disappointment churning within her. "Just thinking about the next move."

They reached the black SUV parked at the curb, its doors yawning open to receive them. As Tom helped Richards into the back seat, Elle paused, staring at the gothic spires of the university. She thought of codes and truths, how each suspect brought them closer to the answer, or further away from it.

"Elle," Tom called, tapping the roof of the car, signaling her to get inside.

"Coming," she answered, tearing her gaze from the ivory tower of academia. She slid into the passenger seat, the leather cool against her skin. The engine roared to life, and the car pulled away, leaving the scene behind them.

CHAPTER SIX

She shot a quick look into the back seat where Richards fidgeted uncomfortably, his breath coming in quick pants. He was fidgeting and shaking his head, moaning as he rocked back and forth.

She continued to study in him in the rearview mirror, attentive, and taking in every detail of his fidgets and groans.

"There's something off about him, Tom," Elle said, her voice low and tinged with concern. She shifted her gaze to her partner, searching for any sign of doubt or skepticism in his eyes.

Tom glanced at her briefly before returning his attention to the road, his grip tightening on the steering wheel. "I know, Elle. But we have to follow the evidence. We can't let our instincts cloud our judgment."

Elle nodded, her mind racing with possibilities. What if they were wrong? What if Richards wasn't involved in the murder they were investigating but instead caught up in something far more sinister? She couldn't shake the feeling that she was missing a crucial piece of the puzzle.

The professor was shaking his head and muttering to himself, rocking back and forth now.

"I didn't hurt anyone!" he called out, his voice strained. "It... it was mutual!"

This sudden outburst seemed like an admission rolled into a justification.

Elle's brow furrowed as she exchanged a glance with Tom. The professor's words hung in the air, heavy with implications. It was a moment of vulnerability, a crack in the facade of fear that revealed a glimpse of truth.

"What do you mean by 'it was mutual'?" Elle asked, her voice steady but her curiosity piqued.

Richards turned to face her, his eyes pleading for understanding amidst the chaos of his own mind. "She wasn't just a victim," he said, his voice now laced with sorrow. "We were involved... intimately involved."

Elle's heart skipped a beat as the puzzle pieces rearranged themselves in her mind. The victim wasn't just another name on a case file; she was someone connected to Richards on a personal level. Suddenly, the motive behind his fear became clearer—it wasn't just about avoiding punishment for murder, but protecting their shared secret.

"Laura Davis?" Elle asked.

"W-what? No. No... no, I... like I said. I barely knew her. I just..."

"You thought we were looking into something else?" Tom said, his voice firm.

"She's an adult!" he retorted. "She can make her own decisions."

"Who was she, Richards?" Elle pressed, her instinct for the truth overriding her usual caution.

Richards hesitated, weighing the consequences of revealing more. But then he seemed to surrender to the inevitability of his situation and leaned back into the seat, defeated. "Her name was Emily," he whispered, his voice choked with emotion. "She was my student. I know you lie… cops lie. It's a trap. I know it is. There is no Laura, is there? This is about Emily?"

Elle blinked, realizing that Richards had ensnared himself in a trap of his own making. The man's active imagination utilized against himself. She didn't reveal this instantly—clearly, his guilty conscience was doing the work for them.

Her hand gripped the windowsill of the car as the vehicle sped up. Her stomach lurched softly as it so often did in vehicles during sudden movements. She consciously forced her mind not to drift to the memories of her parents' accident.

Silence filled the vehicle as Tom and Elle exchanged glances again, their minds racing to make sense of this revelation. A forbidden relationship with a student—such an affair would have had dire consequences for Richards' career and reputation. But could it be enough to drive him to murder? There was still so much they didn't know.

"But I swear," he continued, "I didn't know Laura... I was with Emily the last few nights. She can vouch for me. Her apartment has a camera."

Elle tensed. "Where is this apartment?"

Richards hesitated for a moment, his eyes darting nervously between Elle and Tom. "It's in the city," he finally responded, reluctance evident in his voice. "I can give you the address."

Elle's mind raced with possibilities as she considered Richards' claim. If he could prove that he was with Emily during the time of the murder, it would significantly shift their investigation. But she couldn't let herself be swayed solely by his words. She needed concrete evidence to support his alibi.

"Alright," Elle said, her tone measured yet firm. "We'll need to verify your statement. Tom, let's head to Emily's apartment and see if the camera footage corroborates Richards' story."

Tom nodded and adjusted their course accordingly, the tires of the SUV screeching against the asphalt as they made a sharp turn. The atmosphere inside the car was thick with anticipation and uncertainty—a feeling that mirrored Elle's own conflicted emotions.

But Elle felt as if she already knew how all of this would end up. It troubled her, but her brow was already ridged and furrowed. Her mind was already moving.

The professor had been too quick to provide the alibi. A camera?

He would know how it would cast him if it proved false... no. No, she supposed he was likely telling the truth.

Which meant their next step would take them in another direction.

But where?

She considered this a moment as Tom followed Richards' instructions, only half listening now.

The sister, she finally decided.

Laura Davis had a sister.

If anyone could cast light on this, it might be the sister.

CHAPTER SEVEN

The tires of their unmarked sedan whispered gently against the suburban asphalt, a soothing balm to Elle Keen's frayed nerves. The professor's alibi had checked out.

They'd been forced to process then release him when his lawyer had shown up, but she already knew he wasn't their guy.

No... no, the killer was still out there.

And so their next step had brought them *here.* They rolled past neat lawns and picket fences that seemed worlds away from the yellow tape and flashing police lights they had left behind at the university. She watched as children played on the sidewalks, their laughter floating through the air, untainted by the shadows of crime.

Tom maneuvered the car with a casual ease that belied the tension simmering just beneath his stoic exterior. His hands, large and capable, rested lightly on the steering wheel, and Elle caught herself staring at the pale poppy stitched above his lapel—a stark spot of color against the tailored blue suit that struggled to contain his muscular frame.

"Quiet around here, huh?" Tom's voice was a low rumble, pulling Elle's gaze back to the neighborhood unfurling outside her window.

"Too quiet," Elle murmured, the analytical gears in her mind never ceasing their relentless turn. She glanced over at Tom, taking in the scarred face that somehow added to his rugged charm. His dark eyes remained focused on the road ahead, searching for the address that would lead them to Linda Davis, the sister of the deceased.

Elle felt the contrast keenly; the serenity of this place was a far cry from the chaos of the crime scene. Yet she knew that behind one of these doors lay a link to the brutal reality they were chasing—a reality where Laura Davis had met her end far too soon.

"Here we are," Tom said, as he pulled up to a modest single-story home with cream-colored siding and a welcoming front porch. The garden was well-tended, hydrangeas blooming with vibrant life that stood in defiance of the death that now connected this house to their investigation.

"Let's hope Linda can give us something to work with," Elle said, her voice steady despite the churn of her thoughts.

Tom nodded, his square jaw set with determination. "We'll find who did this, Elle. We owe it to Laura."

With shared resolve, they approached the front door, each step taking them deeper into the heart of Laura Davis's world—a world that held secrets they were desperate to uncover.

Elle's hand hovered over the doorbell, a brief pause to collect her thoughts before pressing it. The sound chimed through the stillness of the suburban afternoon, a gentle disruption in the quiet enclave where grief had taken an inconspicuous seat among the manicured lawns and picket fences.

A moment passed—then another—before the door creaked open. Linda Davis stood there, a phantom of sorrow etched into her features. Her eyes, hollow and seeking, met Elle's with a silent plea for both comfort and answers; answers Elle had come to find but feared she didn't possess.

"Ms. Davis? I'm Agent Elle Keen, and this is my partner, Agent Tom Wright," Elle introduced them with the professional calm she was trained to display, her words a subtle lifeline extended toward Linda's adrift spirit. "We're so sorry to intrude at a time like this, but we need to ask you a few questions about Laura."

Linda nodded mechanically, the gesture betraying the numbness that clung to her like a wet tissue. She stepped aside, allowing them entry. "Of course," her voice was a whisper lost to the silence of the house. "Please, come in."

As they crossed the threshold, Elle took in the home's interior—a shrine to normalcy untouched by the violence that had claimed Laura. The air was thick with the scent of lavender and the faintest hint of freshly baked bread, domestic comforts that now seemed as fragile as glass.

"Can I offer you anything?" Linda asked, her voice barely rising above a hush, as if afraid to disturb the peace her home so desperately clung to.

"No, thank you," Elle declined gently, understanding that the ritual of hospitality offered a semblance of control in a world suddenly slipped from its axis. "We just have a few questions that might help us understand what happened to your sister."

Linda nodded again, her hands wringing together as she led them to a sitting area bathed in the soft glow of the afternoon sun. With each step, Elle felt the weight of responsibility tightening around her—the unspoken promise to unearth truth amidst tragedy, to bring order to chaos with the same meticulous precision she applied to every aspect of her life, a contrast to the unpredictable tempest of a gunfight she so adeptly avoided.

They settled into the living room, and Elle watched as Linda perched on the edge of an armchair, her posture rigid against the plush cushions. It was clear that shock had yet to release its grip, rendering her movements stiff and automatic. Elle chose her words with care, knowing that the echo of gunfire and fear that lingered in her own past was a familiar ghost to those who had lost loved ones too soon.

"Tell us about Laura," Elle began, her tone soft but insistent. "Anything you can think of that might help us catch whoever did this to her."

Linda's voice carried a tremulous note as she began to unravel the threads of Laura's life. "Laura, she... she was always with a book in her hand, from the time we were kids. Shakespeare was her refuge, her passion."

"Which plays did she favor?" Elle asked, her mind already cataloging this detail as potentially significant.

"Her love was constant for 'Hamlet' and 'Macbeth.' She said they spoke to the dualities of human nature," Linda replied, her eyes momentarily brightening with the reflection of Laura's enthusiasm.

"Did she often attend any local theater productions or literature clubs that may have brought her into contact with new people?" Tom chimed in, his question seemingly casual yet pointed.

Linda shook her head slowly. "No, Laura was more private about her hobbies. She preferred the company of her books to crowds. But there was someone... a few weeks ago, she mentioned a man who approached her after a lecture she gave on Elizabethan literature. He made her uncomfortable."

"Can you describe this man?" Elle leaned forward, her dark eyes sharpening with focus.

"Average height, dark hair, and he wore glasses—round, like those old-fashioned ones. He introduced himself as James, but Laura felt there was something off about him. He was insistent on discussing her analysis of 'Othello's' themes of jealousy and betrayal."

"Jealousy and betrayal," Elle echoed, filing away each word like a cipher awaiting decryption. It could be nothing, or it could be the narrative thread they needed to pull.

"Did she meet anyone else who seemed out of place or peculiar?" Elle probed further, aware that every nuance mattered.

"Not that she mentioned," Linda sighed, her fingers absently tracing the floral pattern on the armrest. "Laura kept to herself mostly, even at the university. Her world was her students and her research. She would occasionally attend classes; since she was so young she blended in. But she was fast-tracked. She would make full professor within a few years."

Elle nodded, her mind painting a portrait of Laura Davis—a scholar wrapped in the sanctuary of her literary pursuits, yet not immune to the shadows that lurked beyond the stage's edge. The mention of a stranger named James, the unsettling interest in themes of darkness within humanity's heart, it was a clue worth noting.

"Thank you, Linda," Elle said gently, recognizing the effort it took to sift through memories when grief loomed so large. "Understanding Laura's world helps us understand the threats she might have faced."

As Linda offered a small, appreciative smile, Elle sensed the outline of Laura Davis growing clearer, her existence morphing from abstract victim to flesh and blood—a woman with affections, routines, and fears. With each detail Linda shared, Elle felt the edges of chaos recede, replaced by the beginnings of a pattern only she could see—a code of behavior, preferences, and encounters that might just lead them to a killer hiding behind a curtain of obscurity.

Elle leaned forward, her fingers intertwined as if weaving the threads of the conversation into a tighter pattern. "Linda," she began, her voice carrying the soft cadence of a confidante, "you mentioned Laura's love for literature. Did she often buy books? Perhaps from local stores?"

The question hung in the air for a moment before Linda's expression shifted, a flicker of recognition crossing her features. "Why, yes," she replied, standing up abruptly. "She was always adding to her collection. There's a box of her most recent purchases in the guest room. We buy and sell... or... we *bought* and sold books together. Would you like to see them?"

"Very much so," Elle said, a pulse of anticipation threading through her veins.

Linda disappeared down the corridor, leaving Elle and Tom in the living room that seemed to hold its breath. Tom watched Elle with an appreciative gaze, understanding her tactic—books were more than paper and ink; they were conduits to their owner's psyche.

Moments later, Linda returned, her arms cradling a cardboard container, the edges worn from handling. She set it on the coffee table with reverence. "These are the ones she hadn't gotten around to reading yet."

"Thank you," Elle said, and as Linda retreated to the comfort of her armchair, Elle peered into the box.

She lifted each book, feeling the weight of potential evidence in her hands. Her fingertips danced across the covers, tracing titles and authors, absorbing every iota of information. The sharp intellect that had isolated her in youth now served as her compass in navigating the murky waters of human motives and secrets.

Tom stood aside, watching Elle's process, knowing better than to interrupt her meticulous examination. She was looking for patterns, for the missing piece in the puzzle that Laura's life had become.

Her eyes moved up from the books, and she remained quiet, still taking it all in.

Elle paced the room, her gaze sweeping over the modest surroundings. The walls were painted a calming shade of eggshell, adorned with family portraits smiling down from their perches. She paused before a collection of candid shots, the frozen moments depicting a life that once was—birthday celebrations, holiday gatherings, and sun-drenched vacations. The corners of her mouth twitched involuntarily; such normality seemed out of place given the shadow of tragedy that now loomed over this family.

Her attention shifted to a pile of recently read books stacked neatly on the lower shelf of a coffee table.

"Those were Laura's too!" Linda volunteered, noticing Elle's attention.

Elle crouched down for a better look, her fingers brushing against the spines, each title a silent testament to Laura's varied tastes. Elle noted the absence of dust, evidence of frequent handling, or perhaps a meticulous cleanliness that felt at odds with the chaos they had witnessed earlier in the day.

"Thank you," Elle said, replying a few moments too late for normal conversational rhythms. But she was distracted, her tone more subdued than before. With deliberate care, she reached for the topmost book, a hardback with a glossy cover. She flipped through the pages, noting the crispness, the spine barely creased. Each book yielded similar results—unread, untouched by the eyes for which they'd been intended.

She frowned at this and straightened once more. Linda was staring off, distracted. Elle shared a look with Tom. The two of them thanked Linda for her hospitality and then moved back towards the door.

Elle stepped out onto the porch, a soft click sounding as Linda closed the door behind her. The air was cooler now, shadows lengthening as the day neared its end.

Her eyes scanned the quiet suburban street, where children's laughter echoed from a nearby yard, a stark reminder of life moving forward around the stillness of loss. It was here, in this ordinary setting, that Laura Davis's story had paused, suspended in a mystery that Elle was determined to solve.

"Anything?" Tom's voice pulled Elle back from her thoughts.

She shook her head, her lips pressed into a thin line. "Not what we hoped for," she admitted, her voice carrying that blunt edge she couldn't always soften. But there was something else—a steeliness that emerged when the trail seemed coldest. "No watermarks on those books. They were barely touched. Seems strange for a book lover."

"Not really," Tom said. "Sometimes, people like that collect the books just for their presence in their home. They don't always read what they buy. Like art pieces on a wall."

"Yet," she added quickly, the single streak of white in her dark hair catching the fading light as she turned to face him. "Patterns emerge in the absence of patterns, too."

Tom nodded, understanding the relentless drive that powered his partner. He'd seen it before—the way she could find threads in the thinnest of leads, how her mind worked tirelessly like some intricate machine built solely for unwinding the puzzles that others found impenetrable.

"Let's grab dinner," he suggested, his attempt at casualness betrayed by a glance towards her bag. "Chinese?"

A ghost of a smile crossed Elle's features, a momentary respite in her otherwise focused demeanor. "Sounds good. But let's get it to go. There's still work to do."

As they walked toward their car, the evening breeze carried away the remnants of conversation from Linda's porch. Elle knew the importance of nourishing the body for the sake of the mind, but even as she contemplated the comfort of familiar flavors, her brain continued to churn, searching for the elusive cipher that would unlock Laura Davis's final act.

She settled into the passenger seat, her gaze lost in the passing scenery, each house another opportunity for secrets hidden behind curtains and doors. Somewhere within the day's findings, she felt certain, lurked an anomaly, a piece misplaced or overlooked.

Elle's mind whirred, sifting through Linda's words, Laura's books, the images and impressions of an unassuming home. Her hunger for truth gnawed at her stronger than any physical appetite. With each turn of the wheels, hope and disappointment mixed within her like a complex code, waiting, begging to be broken. And she would break it, Elle vowed silently. Because codes were truth, and for Agent Elle Keen, truth was everything.

CHAPTER EIGHT

Shadows draped the man like a cloak, rendering him nearly invisible in the remote corner of the bustling theater. His gaze pierced through the dimness, unwavering and intense as it locked onto the figure at center stage—a woman radiating vitality under the spotlight. Sarah Mason, her name etched in his mind as indelibly as the lines she recited.

The rehearsal thrummed with life, actors animated in their timeless dance of dialogue and drama, but all he saw was Juliet—Sarah Mason embodying her with an ethereal grace that transcended the wooden planks of the stage. She moved with a fluidity that spoke of youth and love, her voice lilting through the verses of Shakespeare with an ease that belied the complexity of the emotions she portrayed.

He took mental notes, each nuance of her performance etching deeper into his consciousness. The way the fabric of her Elizabethan gown hugged her form, the subtle gesture of her hand reaching towards her imaginary Romeo, the delicate tilt of her head as she delivered her lines—all were details that fascinated the killer. Sarah Mason, in her portrayal of Juliet, had become the unwitting muse to his dark obsession.

The vibrant tapestry of 'Romeo and Juliet' unfolded before him, yet in his mind's eye, it was not Verona that came alive, but a more sinister stage set for a different kind of finale. He savored the irony of the play’s tragic themes interweaving with his own intentions. As Sarah's voice rose and fell with Shakespeare's metered rhythm, he felt himself drawn further into the fantasy he was crafting—one where he, too, could direct a scene that would be immortalized in infamy.

The rehearsal hall echoed with the final notes of a lovesick melody as Sarah Mason's portrayal of Juliet transitioned from the light-hearted flutterings of newfound love to the heavy, soul-baring torment of impending loss. The man watched, concealed in shadow, as she gazed upward, her eyes shimmering with unshed tears, embodying the very essence of Shakespeare’s tragic heroine.

"O serpent heart, hid with a flowering face!" Her voice broke through the hush of the auditorium, each syllable a testament to Juliet's betrayal and anguish. He leaned forward slightly, his breath caught between fascination and a darker, pulsing excitement. How effortlessly she captured the duality of innocence and devastation—qualities he found most appealing for his macabre designs.

Sarah continued, unfurling the soliloquy with a vulnerability that made the air thrum with tension. "Was ever book containing such vile matter so fairly bound?" The killer felt a surge of satisfaction; Juliet's lament over Romeo's banishment mirrored the twisted narrative he had composed in his mind. She was not just reciting lines; she was breathing life into them—a life he yearned to extinguish in homage to her artistry.

As she reached the crescendo of her soliloquy, the hall erupted in applause. The killer barely registered the sound. To him, it was as distant as the rustle of leaves outside the safety of his darkened alcove. His focus remained tethered to Sarah, to the raw emotion she spilled forth on stage, an emotion that seeped into his veins, igniting a frenzy within his twisted psyche.

"Thou piteous thing," she whispered, the final words hanging in the air like a prayer for mercy. And even as the clapping continued, all he heard were the echoes of Juliet's despair mingling with the silent symphony of his anticipation. For in those delicate moments of theatrical tragedy, Sarah Mason had unknowingly auditioned for a role in his own perverse production—one she was destined to play.

Pen poised over a leather-bound notebook, the man's eyes never left Sarah as she delivered Juliet's heart-wrenching lament. The dim light of the theater barely reached his corner, yet it glinted off his watchful gaze, reflecting a mind that wove dark parallels between the staged tragedy and his own impending design. Every nuance in Sarah's portrayal was a thread in the tapestry of the finale he envisioned for her—a finale not penned by Shakespeare, but by his own hand.

He scribbled furiously now, each word etching itself into the fabric of his plan. Sarah's costume—a gown of deep crimson, its bodice embroidered with golden threads—was noted with an artist's precision. He imagined how it would look under different lighting, how the color would contrast starkly with the pallor of Sarah's skin once he had directed her last scene.

"O happy dagger," Sarah cried out, clutching the prop to her chest, "This is thy sheath." The killer watched, rapt, as she mimicked Juliet's final act of devotion, her voice quivering with feigned despair. Her dialogue, memorized by so many, took on a new, sinister significance as he transcribed it into his notebook, punctuating each line with his own silent annotations.

"Rust, and let me die," she concluded, collapsing onto the stage with a grace that belied the violence of the act. The man's fingers traced the words he had written, a blueprint for what was to come. In his twisted vision, he saw Sarah's performance not as a culmination of her craft, but as a rehearsal for the role she was yet to unknowingly play—the star of his morbid reenactment, where the curtain call would be final, and the applause, forever absent.

In the dim glow of the theater's stage lights, her soliloquy ended, and he could feel his heartbeat quicken. With each actor's bow and the audience's applause fading into a distant murmur, his focus sharpened on Sarah Mason alone. The roses—that would be the final touch. In his mind, the scene played out with cinematic precision: Sarah, still adorned in her crimson gown, lying motionless upon a bed of the most exquisite red petals, each one an offering to this twisted shrine he would erect.

The very thought sent a shiver through him, but it was not of revulsion; it was pure exhilaration. He imagined the fragrance of the roses overwhelming the senses, just as the sight of her would overwhelm the soul—a juxtaposition of beauty and horror that would carve his work into the annals of infamy.

His pulse thrummed with the intensity of his anticipation, an artist envisioning the climax of his greatest creation. Not a mere killer, no—such a term was too crude, too banal for the likes of him. He was the playwright of this macabre drama, choreographing the final scene where love and death would dance in a perverse pas de deux. This surge of adrenaline fuelled his deranged fantasies, each beat of his heart a drumroll leading to the grand finale he yearned to orchestrate.

His eyes clung to her figure, tracing the soft contours of Sarah's form as she laughed with fellow actors. The cacophony of their camaraderie was a distant hum in his ears, their joyous ignorance a veil through which only he could see the stark truth of impending finality. He memorized the curve of her smile, the way her hair cascaded down her shoulders—details that would soon be immortalized through his design.

With the stealth of a shadow, he edged backward into the dimly lit corridor, each step deliberate and silent. His presence dissolved into the darkness, as ephemeral as the ghost light that would soon stand sentinel on the empty stage. The door closed with a whisper, severing him from the world within—a world that remained blissfully unaware of the predator that had just departed from their midst.

As the cool night air embraced him, his heart pounded with a composer's rhythm against the cage of his chest. Each breath he drew was laced with the electricity of anticipation; every fiber of his being vibrated with the knowledge that soon, the lines between the play and reality would blur irreversibly. He walked, but it was not a man's gait; it was the measured strides of destiny approaching.

And there, under the cloak of darkness, he allowed himself a small, satisfied smile. The streets were quiet, the city unsuspecting, as he vanished like a specter into the night—carrying with him the chilling thrill of a story about to unfold not on the boards of a stage, but in the stark prose of life itself. Soon, very soon, fiction would breathe its first breath of reality.

CHAPTER NINE

The first light of dawn cast a pale glow over the decrepit facade of Rebecca Grey's old studio as Elle and Tom stepped out of their unmarked car.

Morning, and a night's rest, provided new perspective, and now the two of them had convinced their supervisor to bundle the two cases.

They were officially leads on the literature killer's case. As they approached the old studio where the first victim from nearly a month ago had resided, Elle shifted uncomfortably, taking in the structure before them.

The building, a somber relic of artistic glory now surrendered to time, stood quietly in the morning stillness, its windows like blind eyes to the world outside.

"Looks like it hasn't seen life in ages," Tom murmured, his voice a low rumble that seemed almost invasive in the quiet of the morning.

Elle nodded, her gaze fixed on the peeling paint and the cobwebs festooning the corners of the entrance. "A perfect scene for a mystery novel," she thought, acknowledging the eerie tranquility with a mix of reverence and melancholy.

With each step up the creaky stairs, Elle felt the weight of the past thickening the air around them. She reached out, her fingers tracing the contours of the once-vibrant sign by the door—now faded to obscurity. Pushing open the heavy wooden door, its hinges protesting with a groan, Elle and Tom crossed the threshold into what was once Rebecca's sanctuary.

As they entered, particles of dust swirled lazily in the shafts of sunlight piercing through the broken blinds. The room lay in a state of arrested decay, canvases haphazardly strewn about, tubes of paint dried and cracked, and brushes stiff with forgotten strokes. Every surface was coated in a fine layer of dust, untouched since the day Rebecca had taken her last breath within these walls.

"Feels like a tomb," Elle remarked, her voice barely above a whisper, unwilling to disturb the sacred silence that had settled over the room.

Tom nodded solemnly, his eyes scanning the chaotic harmony of art and entropy. "If these walls could talk," he said, glancing at Elle. His scarred face, usually so impassive, was softened in the half-light, giving him an almost ethereal quality.

"Let's hope they'll speak to us today," Elle replied. Her analytical mind began cataloging the room, each detail a potential cipher waiting to be decoded. She moved slowly, deliberately, her keen eyes catching the way the dust motes danced around a paint-splattered easel, or how the light played off the metallic frame of an old, tarnished mirror.

"Imagine the stories," Tom added, running his hand along a canvas, leaving a streak in the dust, revealing a vibrant color beneath—a stark reminder of the life that once pulsed through this space.

"Every masterpiece has its secrets," Elle mused aloud, her thoughts drifting back to her own parents' mystery, the insatiable need for answers driving her forward. She found herself drawn to a small table, where personal effects lay frozen in time: a mug with a ring of dried coffee, a tattered sketchbook, and scattered notes penned in haste.

"Time stopped here," she said, looking up at Tom, her prematurely white-streaked hair catching a stray beam of light, "but we're going to start it up again." Her conviction was palpable, fueling their quest for truth amidst the silent testament of Rebecca's life and untimely demise.

Elle's fingers brushed against the rough texture of a canvas, her touch cautious as if the painted surface might crumble under too firm a grip. The studio was a graveyard of inspiration, where every corner seemed to hold whispered echoes of Rebecca Grey's creative fervor. Tom moved methodically on the other side of the room, lifting sheets of dust-covered plastic from props and furniture, his presence a reassuring constant in the otherwise eerie stillness.

"Anything?" Elle called out, her voice barely above a whisper, unwilling to disturb the hallowed quiet.

"Nothing yet," Tom responded, shaking his head. He held up a stack of photographs, their edges curled and yellowed with age. "Just memories."

Elle turned back to the canvases, aligning them with precision. She knew that patterns often lurked beneath chaos, her life's experiences had taught her that much. And like the cryptic crosswords she solved to unwind, she recognized that every element before her could be a clue.

She paused, her gaze landing on a half-finished painting that stood apart from the rest—a striking image of a young man, handsome and arrogant, draped in finery, the background an ominous shade that seemed to drip with foreboding. It was 'The Picture of Dorian Gray', the portrait incomplete, the subject's eyes hauntingly blank, as if staring into an abyss.

"Tom, look at this," she said, her voice tinged with a newfound urgency. He joined her, and together they peered at the artwork.

"Rebecca was working on Dorian Gray," Elle murmured, her mind racing. "Laura's house... the copy of Hamlet we found—it can't be a coincidence."

"An artist and a bibliophile," Tom mused, his brow furrowed in thought. "Both killed, and both with a literary twist to their final scene."

"Exactly." Elle stepped closer to the painting, her eyes scanning the brushstrokes for any sign of deviation, any hint that might lead them closer to understanding.

"Rebecca's work here," she gestured to the painting, "it's personal, passionate. If our killer is truly obsessed with literature, maybe he saw himself in these stories."

"Or wanted to rewrite them," Tom added, his gaze not leaving the unfinished eyes of Dorian.

"Let's photograph everything. We need to document each piece, especially this one." Elle pulled out her camera, capturing the painting from multiple angles, her movements precise and calculated.

As she looked once more at the unfinished Dorian, Elle felt a shiver run down her spine, a silent communion with the past. Whoever had taken Rebecca's life had left more than just a body; they had left a message woven into the very fabric of her art.

***

The gravel crunched beneath the tires of their unmarked sedan as Elle and Tom followed the winding driveway flanked by fields of wildflowers. The serenity of the countryside, with its sprawling meadows and the distant chorus of birdsong, stood in stark contrast to the chaos of the city they had left behind. Elle's gaze rested on the horizon where the dawn had painted the sky in hues of orange and pink, a gentle reminder that the world was still turning, despite the darkness they were chasing.

"Quite a change from Rebecca's studio," Tom mused, his eyes taking in the rustic charm of the old farmhouse ahead.

"Her parents chose seclusion over the limelight," Elle replied, her mind already canvassing for clues that might thread through the tranquility of this secluded life.

They parked beside an ancient oak tree whose roots seemed to burrow deep into the earth, much like the family secrets they hoped to unearth. Elle stepped out, her boots sinking slightly into the dew-covered grass. She straightened her blazer, brushed a leaf from her hair, and prepared herself mentally for the conversation ahead.

"Ready?" Tom asked, checking his reflection in the car window and smoothing down his tie.

"I guess," she responded, though her heart was pounding slightly faster than usual. Interactions like these were unpredictable—every word, every inflection could either open doors or shut them tight.

Together, they approached the farmhouse, its white paint peeling slightly from years of facing the elements. A wind chime tinkled softly, the sound oddly soothing amidst the tension of their task.

Tom raised his hand and knocked firmly on the wooden door, the sound echoing slightly in the morning calm. As they waited, Elle observed the minutiae of the place: the well-tended garden beds, the curtains that fluttered lightly from an upstairs window, the faint aroma of baking bread wafting through the air.

Moments later, the door creaked open, revealing the weathered faces of Rebecca Grey's parents, lines etched by both time and grief. Their eyes held a mixture of curiosity and wariness as they regarded the two agents standing before them.

"Mr. and Mrs. Grey?" Elle began, showing her badge. "We're very sorry to disturb you, but we have a few questions about your daughter."

The couple exchanged a glance, a silent conversation passing between them before they stepped aside to welcome Elle and Tom into their home. As they crossed the threshold, Elle couldn't help but feel the weight of the past pressing in around them, each room a potential vessel of truth waiting to be unlocked.

Elle took a seat at the old oak dining table, its surface polished by years of hands passing over it. Tom settled across from her, his posture careful, respectful. The room was warm, suffused with the golden glow of morning light filtering through lace curtains. Mrs. Grey poured tea into delicate china cups, her motions practiced, while Mr. Grey sat down stiffly, his hands clasped tightly on the table.

"Rebecca always loved a good story," Mrs. Grey began, her voice soft but clear, breaking the brief silence. "Ever since she was a little girl, she'd spend hours in her room, reading. We thought she'd become a writer one day."

"Or an artist," Mr. Grey added, casting a wistful glance towards a framed photograph on the mantelpiece—a younger Rebecca, palette in hand, beaming beside a canvas. "She had a passion for the classics—Shakespeare, Austen, Wilde. She found beauty in their words and translated it onto her canvases."

Elle nodded, sipping her tea to hide a momentary lapse as she considered this new thread connecting Rebecca to Laura Davis, who had also been enamored with literature and art. It wasn't just a mere coincidence—it was a pattern emerging, a shared trait between the victims that could be vital to their investigation.

"Her work was remarkable," Elle commented, setting down her cup. Her gaze shifted to the Greys. "In the time before her death, did Rebecca mention anything unusual? Any odd encounters or someone who might have taken her interest in literature too far?"

The question hung in the air like a dark cloud threatening rain. Mrs. Grey's hands paused, a tremor betraying her composure. Mr. Grey's jaw tightened, and he exchanged a look with his wife that Elle read as protective, fear laced within the silent communication.

"Rebecca never spoke of threats," Mrs. Grey finally said, her voice thinner now. "But there was an intensity around her last few months...a fervor in her work that seemed driven by something more than inspiration."

"Driven how?" Tom interjected gently.

"Obsession, perhaps," Mr. Grey murmured, a distant frown creasing his brow. "Her art consumed her, more so near the end. She'd be up all night painting, muttering about deadlines that didn't exist."

"Deadlines..." Elle echoed, pondering the implications. Obsession could be a motive, a catalyst. Or perhaps it was something else—an external pressure they hadn't yet uncovered.

"Thank you," Elle said with genuine warmth, standing up. "You've given us much to consider." She glanced at Tom, who gave a subtle nod.

"May I look in Rebecca's old room?"

"Her... she doesn't live here... I mean, didn't..." but then the mother shrugged and nodded. "Upstairs, first door."

Elle nodded gratefully, leaving Tom to soothe the grieving couple. She approached the stairs, taking them two at a time, her eyes scanning every detail she spotted.

Elle pushed open the door to Rebecca's childhood room, its hinges protesting with a drawn-out creak. The space seemed frozen in time, dust motes dancing in the sunbeams that filtered through the gauzy curtains. With each step she took, the floorboards whispered secrets of a past long gone.

"Feels like walking into a time capsule," Elle murmured to herself, scanning the room filled with vintage posters and dog-eared books that lined the shelves. "Or a crypt," Elle added softly, her eyes narrowing as they landed on a book splayed open on the desk, its pages yellowed with age. She moved toward it, a sense of purpose sharpening her focus. It was an annotated copy of 'The Picture of Dorian Gray', the margins littered with handwritten notes and scribbles.

She traced a finger over the annotations, each word a breadcrumb leading them deeper into the labyrinth of the case. Rebecca didn't just love literature; she lived it. And these notes...

Elle's thoughts paused, and she frowned, leaning down and flipping a page.

She stared... A strange watermark.

This one, though, hadn't been ruined by a bathtub and blood. This one she could read.

She spoke aloud, the words on her tongue. *Emma Wilson Books.*

A book store. She frowned. The watermark was placed in the exact spot as the one from the previous crime scene.

A coincidence?

Even the ink looked the same.

She shivered, taking a photograph of the watermark. She scanned the annotations now, realizing that the handwriting was different in some sections. Not all of these were Rebecca's notes. Someone had owned the book before.

Emma Wilson?

Someone else obsessed with literature?

Elle frowned, her finger tracing the pages of the book.

As she continued to examine the annotated pages, Elle's mind raced with possibilities. What if Emma Wilson was not just an innocent book lover but a person connected to these crimes? Could she be the missing link between the victims, the common thread that would unravel the mystery?

Determined to find answers, Elle pocketed the photograph of the watermark and carefully closed the book. She needed to pay a visit to Emma Wilson Books and dig deeper into this connection. The bookstore might hold the key to unlocking the truth behind these gruesome murders.

With renewed focus, Elle descended the stairs and found Tom still speaking with Rebecca's parents. Their eyes mirrored the pain of losing their daughter, but Elle could see a glimmer of hope in their faces as she approached.

"Thank you for allowing me to look through Rebecca's room," Elle said sincerely, her gaze lingering on the Greys. "I believe I've found something significant."

Mrs. Grey's eyes widened with anticipation. "What is it? Did you discover something that could help find the person responsible for our daughter's death?"

Elle nodded, her voice steady and determined. "I believe there's a connection between Rebecca and another person, but I can't discuss them just yet. I found a book in her room with annotations, though. Was your daughter the note-taking sort?"

Mrs. Grey furrowed her brow, deep in thought. "Rebecca was always meticulous," she said, her voice tinged with a mix of pride and sadness. "She would underline passages, scribble notes, and jot down ideas that struck her while reading."

"Would she borrow someone else's annotated books?'

"I...Maybe, but I don't recall her ever mentioning anyone else's annotations or borrowing someone else's book."

Elle's curiosity intensified. If the handwriting in the book didn't belong to Rebecca, who could it be? And how did it connect to Emma Wilson Books? She needed to find out more, piece the puzzle together.

Mrs. Grey's eyes glistened with tears as she nodded. "Rebecca was always taking notes. She had a thirst for knowledge, a hunger to understand everything she read. It was one of the things we loved most about her."

Elle's heart clenched at the mother's words, a pang of empathy washing over her. "Thank you for sharing that with me," she said softly, placing a gentle hand on Mrs. Grey's shoulder. "I believe these annotations might hold the key to uncovering the truth behind Rebecca's death—and potentially the other victim as well."

Mr. Grey leaned forward, his voice filled with desperation. "Please, Agent Keen, tell us everything you know. We need to find justice for our daughter."

Elle took a deep breath, her mind racing as she formulated her response. These grieving parents deserved answers, and she was determined to find them. "The annotations in Rebecca's book led me to a connection—a watermark that matches one found at another crime scene," she explained, her voice steady and resolute.

"A connection?" Tom interjected, furrowing his brow. "What do you mean?"

Elle met Tom's gaze and then turned back to the Greys. "I believe there is another person involved in these crimes—a person who shares

Rebecca's passion for literature," she began carefully, choosing her words with precision. "This person might be using books as a way to connect with their victims or leave behind clues."

Mrs. Grey gasped, clutching her husband's hand tightly as realization dawned on her face. "You mean... someone who knew our daughter?"

"We'll see. I wish I could say more. But for now, let us do our jobs. I promise to do what I can."

The parents watched her, but then looked at each other, and it was as if their attention vanished, turning on one another instead.

Elle shared a glance with Tom and nodded towards the door.

He murmured a few consoling words as they both prepared to leave. Elle felt a bolt of sympathy, but she wasn't the sort to properly offer commiseration. Her way with words wasn't what made her a good agent.

No... The way she'd help the grieving couple was to find the person responsible.

And right now, that road led directly to Emma Wilson's bookstore.

CHAPTER TEN

All roads led to Emma Wilson, and now, Elle could feel the tension mounting as they drew closer to their target.

The city's relentless hum faded as Elle and Tom turned down an alley that seemed to unravel into another era. Brick buildings with fire escapes zigzagging across their faces narrowed the sky to a slit of pale blue. At the alley's end, wedged between a pawnshop with barred windows and a bodega overflowing with ripe fruit stands, stood Emma Wilson's bookstore, titled simply *Emma Wilson's Books.*

"Here we are," Elle murmured, her gaze tracing the gold-leaf lettering on the weathered sign that hung by a single, creaking chain.

"Looks like it hasn't seen a fresh coat of paint in decades," Tom observed, his deep voice resonating against the alley walls. His dark eyes swept over the display window where books lay stacked haphazardly, their spines sun-bleached and pages yellowed with time.

"Maybe not, but there's history here. Stories wrapped in stories," she replied, stepping closer to the glass, her breath fogging up a small circle on the pane. A book with a faded cover caught her eye—a first edition, she noted, the kind collectors would pay dearly for.

Tom pushed the door open, and a bell jangled, announcing their arrival. The scent of old paper and leather-bound volumes enveloped them, a sharp contrast to the city's exhaust fumes and asphalt just yards away.

"Time to see what Emma Wilson's part in all this is," Elle said more to herself than to Tom. Her eyes scanned the bookshelves, taking in the numbers and letters marking the shelves and distinguishing them from one another. Like license plates or phone numbers, Elle was capable of remembering digits within seconds of seeing them.

They stepped into the literary labyrinth, ready to untangle the next thread of the mystery that had led them here.

The chime of the entrance bell faded into the dense, book-laden air as Elle and Tom ventured deeper into the heart of Emma Wilson's realm. Shelves bowed under the weight of countless stories, the musty aroma of aging paper wrapping around them like an old quilt. Elle's eyes sharpened on the scene before her—books stacked in teetering piles, titles jammed together with little regard for genre or author.

"Quite the eclectic collection," Tom mumbled, thumbing through a volume of poetry wedged between a dog-eared spy thriller and a thick tome on European history.

"Or a reflection of a mind that can't quite keep things straight," Elle countered quietly, noting the chaos that surrounded her. It was as if each shelf was a puzzle piece to Emma's psyche, the disorder speaking volumes more than the books themselves could ever whisper.

A creak echoed from behind the counter, dragging their attention to the shopkeeper. Emma Wilson emerged, her presence understated yet unmistakable. A frizzy halo of red hair framed her pale face, and her cardigan hung off her shoulders like an afterthought. Her hands clung to one another as she approached, fingers betraying a tremble.

"Detectives," she greeted, her voice laced with the crackle of dry leaves, suggesting a parched throat or age beyond her features. "I wasn't expecting company today."

"We're just looking for some answers," Elle replied, locking onto Emma's gaze. She noted how the woman's eyes flitted nervously, not quite meeting hers, instead darting to a shadowed corner where the classics held court over modern tales.

"Of course, ask away." Emma gestured to the chaos around her, an attempt at nonchalance that didn't quite reach the corners of her strained smile. "But please excuse the mess, I've been meaning to organize..."

"Seems like quite the task," Tom quipped, but his jovial tone failed to mask the underlying scrutiny of his words.

"Indeed," Elle agreed, her observation narrowing as Emma's glance once again stole away to the same section of the store. There was something there, a silent beacon calling to the shopkeeper, and Elle made a mental note to explore that corner thoroughly once they had peeled back a few more layers of Emma Wilson's carefully constructed veneer.

Elle leaned forward, her elbows resting on a stack of haphazardly piled books. "Emma," she began, the pitch of her voice firm yet measured, "you sold books to Laura Davis and Rebecca Gray—books that ended up at their respective crime scenes. What can you tell us about your interactions with them?"

Emma's fingers twitched, tracing the spine of a worn copy of 'Wuthering Heights' as if seeking solace in its tattered pages. "I sell books to hundreds of people. Those names don't ring any bells."

"Yet these very books became part of a murder scene, Emma. That's not just an everyday coincidence," Tom interjected, folding his arms as he watched her closely.

Her eyes darted away, then back, a flicker of knowledge—or was it fear?—flashing through her gaze before she masked it with an overly bright laugh. "I'm sure it's just a bizarre twist of fate. You must see strange connections in your line of work all the time."

"Perhaps," Elle said, voice cool, "but we're more interested in patterns than coincidences. Did either of them mention anything unusual when purchasing from you? Any particular interest in certain themes or authors?"

Elle pushed on. She'd come in guns blazing, but it had been intentional. Someone who didn't know about the murders might've reacted in shock or fear. They might've thrown their hands up in surprise or gasped as they stumbled back.

But none of these reactions were found in Emma's countenance. She looked nervous, but rehearsed, as if attempting to keep herself calm.

She knew about the case... Knew about the victims.

Elle didn't try to give her the out. Rather, she pushed on as if it were a foregone conclusion the bookstore owner *knew* these women.

"YOu must remember them. Laura Davis and Rebecca Gray. Tell us about them, please."

Not *can* you tell us. Or *will* you tell us? But *tell* us. A demand.

It required an answer.

Neither Tom nor Elle blinked, both of them staring at the frizzy-haired, nervous bookstore owner.

Emma clasped and unclasped her hands, a bead of perspiration visible on her brow despite the chill lingering between the overstocked shelves. "I... right... okay, yes. I think I remember now. Laura was quiet, reserved. She loved the classics, said they spoke to her in a way modern novels couldn't. And Rebecca—she came in occasionally, always in a hurry, always asking for recommendations on dark romances or tragic tales."

Elle noticed the subtle shift in Emma's posture, the way she leaned slightly towards the counter as though yearning for a barrier between herself and their questions. "Interesting choices. It seems to me that someone who enjoys those genres might also appreciate the significance of their role in a crime narrative," she mused aloud.

"Speculation isn't evidence, Agent Keen," Emma countered quickly, too quickly, her voice rising an octave in her eagerness to dismiss the implication. "I love those stories, too, but that doesn't make me a murderer!"

"Nobody's calling you a murderer, Emma," Elle reassured, observing the frantic dance of Emma's fidgeting fingers. "But your connection to both victims is peculiar. We're trying to understand the link."

Emma exhaled, a shallow, shaky breath, and pressed her palms against the surface of her cluttered counter, as if grounding herself. "I don't know what else you want me to say. I didn't really know them."

"Yet you remember selling to them," Elle pointed out, watching as Emma's nervous glance strayed once more, a silent siren call only she could hear.

Elle moved through the aisles of the bookstore like a shadow trailing a suspect, her eyes never straying far from Emma. The bookseller's gaze kept flickering to an alcove partially obscured by a standing shelf overstocked with thrillers and crime novels. With each nervous glance that darted away from Elle, Emma unwittingly beckoned her closer to that particular corner.

"Tom, cover me," Elle whispered without looking back, knowing her partner would understand. She sidestepped a pile of leather-bound classics precariously balanced on the floor and approached the secluded section.

Tom stepped forward, obscuring Emma's view and engaging her in more questioning.

The air grew denser with the musty scent of aged paper as Elle neared the alcove. Shelves bowed under the weight of literature that had been thumbed through by countless readers, but here, in this curated corner, there was order amidst chaos. A brass placard declared it 'The Shrine of Tragic Flaws'.

Elle's eyes swept over the spines, and two titles leapt out at her: 'The Picture of Dorian Gray' and 'Hamlet'. They were displayed prominently, their covers free of dust, unlike the others—an indication of frequent handling. Oscar Wilde and Shakespeare watched over the section like patron saints of human folly.

"Curious her interest in these tales," Elle murmured to herself, her fingers grazing the edge of Dorian Gray's ornate cover. Thoughts raced behind her dark walnut eyes as she pieced together fragments of possibility. The victims had been found with copies of these exact books—a coincidence too stark to overlook.

"Agent Keen?" Tom's voice brought her back from the precipice of her thoughts. "Did you find something?" he asked, his figure appearing around the corner, a silent sentinel alert to every nuance.

"Maybe," Elle replied, still examining the books. "These titles... they're linked to our victims. They look like a popular commodity here."

"Could one of them be leaving us breadcrumbs? A signature?" Tom pondered, his brow furrowing.

"Or a red herring," Elle countered, her analytical mind turning over every scenario. "We need concrete evidence."

"Her alibi just came in." Tom held up his phone, the backlight casting shadows across his face. "She was incarcerated during Rebecca's murder."

Elle blinked. "W-what?"

Tom shrugged, turning the phone towards Elle. "An environmental rally that went overboard. She was caught blocking traffic. Spent two nights in jail."

He showed her the mugshot of the frizzy-haired bookstore owner.

"Jail," Elle echoed, feeling the tight grip of the puzzle loosen slightly, only to present new enigmas. "That rules her out for Rebecca, but what about Laura?"

"Still a possibility," Tom nodded. "But we can't ignore this."

Elle's gaze swept from the cluttered bookshelves to Emma Wilson, whose fingers nervously toyed with a tattered bookmark. The musty scent of old paper filled the air as silence stretched between them.

She returned to the bookstore owner, frowning.

"Emma," Elle began, her voice steady despite the whirlwind of thoughts, "your connections to both Laura and Rebecca can't be ignored."

"I've told you everything I know, Agent Keen," Emma insisted, but her eyes flitted once again to the section of classics, betraying an undercurrent of fear or perhaps knowledge she wasn't sharing.

Elle studied her, the analytical gears in her mind churning. Emma's behavior was peppered with red flags, yet the alibi stood firm—a wall blocking the path to a straightforward accusation. Elle could almost hear the silent hum of code strings falling into place, but this time the sequence didn't add up to guilt.

"I... I mean, I guess I remember *something,*" she said quickly.

Elle stared.

Wilson cleared her throat, leaned back and shrugged. "I think... Laura. Yes... she was... she seemed antsy. Upset about something the last time she was in."

"Do you remember what she purchased?"

"I'm afraid not."

"Do you have a record of it?"

"Most of my customers prefer cash. They get discounts that way."

Elle frowned. "She was nervous?"

"It was subtle," Emma said slowly, "But I remember it because

it was out of character for her. She was usually so composed and friendly, but that day, she seemed on edge. I asked if everything was alright, and she brushed it off, saying she was just having a rough day."

Elle's mind raced, trying to piece together the puzzle. Laura's anxiety and Emma's evasiveness were significant pieces of information, but they still didn't provide a clear motive or lead. She needed more.

"Emma, do you have any security footage from that day?" Elle asked, her voice gentle yet persistent.

Emma hesitated before saying, "Yes, I have cameras installed in the store. Let me pull up the footage for you."

As Emma disappeared into the back room, Elle turned to Tom, who had been listening intently. "If we're lucky, the security footage might give us some answers," she said.

Tom nodded in agreement. "Let's hope it does. Maybe we'll find something that will lead us closer to the suspect."

"So we're ruling Emma out?"

"Jail is a pretty good alibi," Tom muttered under his breath. "We can keep a unit on her, just in case."

Seconds later, Emma returned with a small laptop in her hands. She opened it up and began searching through the footage. The screen flickered for a moment before displaying an image from the day Laura had visited the bookstore.

Elle leaned in closer, studying the grainy image. Laura stood at the counter, her body tense, as she paid for her purchase. Emma handed her a brown paper bag containing the book while Laura looked nervously over her shoulder.

Elle's eyes widened as she noticed a figure lurking in the background—a man wearing a dark coat and a hat pulled low over his face. He seemed to be watching Laura intently.

"Who's this?" Elle asked, pointing towards the figure.

Emma leaned in. "Huh... I... I don't know."

Elle's mind raced, trying to make sense of the mysterious figure in the security footage. She glanced at Tom, who was studying the image with a furrowed brow.

"Do you recognize him?" Elle asked Emma, her eyes never leaving the screen.

Emma shook her head. "I've never seen him before. He certainly wasn't a regular customer."

Tom spoke up, his voice laced with concern. "We need to find out who he is. He might be our missing link."

Elle nodded in agreement. "Emma, do you have any other security cameras in the vicinity? Maybe we can track his movements."

Emma's eyes darted around nervously. "Yes, there's another camera outside the store. It captures the parking lot and part of the street."

"Great," Elle said, her excitement building. "Let's check that footage as well. Maybe we can trace his steps and figure out where he came from or where he went."

Emma quickly retrieved another laptop and connected it to the monitor displaying the previous footage. Moments later, another video clip played, showing the view from the external camera.

Elle's heart skipped a beat as she saw the mysterious man step out of a black sedan parked across the street. He glanced around cautiously before crossing over to Laura's car and tampering with something underneath it.

"That's it!" Elle exclaimed, her eyes shining with determination. "He planted something on Laura's car."

Tom leaned closer to get a better look. "Could be some kind of tracking device."

Elle turned to Emma, her voice steady but urgent. "Send this footage to us, please."

"S-sure..."

Elle was staring at the image, frowning. If the killer had used a tracking device, it meant that he didn't likely know where his victim lived. This widened the potential pool of suspects. The man in the video kept his brim low, and his large coat covering his frame. There were no telltale signs. It would take a team meticulously pouring over the footage to glean any information.

As Emma hurriedly processed the footage to send their way, Elle steadied herself, releasing a slow, pent-up breath.

"Thank you for your cooperation," Elle said to Emma with a nod, though her eyes remained sharp, missing nothing. "We'll be in touch if we have more questions."

Emma only nodded, clasping her hands together as if to still their trembling.

Stepping out onto the sidewalk, the city noise rushed to greet them—a stark contrast to the hushed confines of the bookstore they left behind. Elle pulled her coat tighter around her as an autumn chill nipped at her cheeks.

"Another dead end?" Tom asked, his breath forming clouds in the crisp air.

"With Emma, yes. But that guy... He's the one," Elle murmured, her mind refusing to shut down, continuously sifting through data and human puzzles. She replayed Emma's reactions, the layout of the bookstore, the specific titles that had caught her attention. Every detail was another digit in the code, yet the message remained elusive.

"Let's grab some dinner; you need to eat," Tom suggested, glancing at Elle with mild concern.

"Chinese sounds good," Elle responded automatically, her favorite comfort unable to lift the veil of mystery that clouded her thoughts.

As they walked down the bustling street, the day's fading light cast long shadows that seemed to mock their lack of progress. But Elle knew better than to retreat into the darkness of uncertainty. Tomorrow was another day in the cipher of crime, and she would be ready, codes and all, to delve deeper into the labyrinth they had stumbled upon.

They would send the footage to the lab, have it graded up, and then meticulously examine.

Something would stand out.

It had to.

CHAPTER ELEVEN

The lock clicked shut behind Elle with a soft snick that echoed through the silence of her apartment. She leaned back against the door for a moment, the weight of the day pressing down on her like the heavy tomes of code that filled her bookshelves. Her home was less living space, more command center—a reflection of her relentless drive—a menagerie of blinking lights and whirring machines, each one a soldier in her personal army against disorder.

Her fingers deftly untangled from the straps of her bag as she shrugged it off, the leather thudding to the floor amidst the scattered islands of case files. The room was dark, save for the pale glow of streetlamps filtering through the blinds, casting long, angular shadows across the teetering piles of paperwork and cutting-edge tech gadgets that were strewn about.

Elle's mind raced, synthesizing the day's revelations, her thoughts a torrent of codes and ciphers, victims' faces, and the killer's elusive shadow. She navigated the familiar maze of her apartment with ease, sidestepping a stack of books without looking, her body moving on autopilot while her brain worked overtime.

With a flick of a switch, the room was bathed in the sterile light of fluorescents, revealing the chaos of her obsession. Her gaze swept over the organized disarray, a physical manifestation of the puzzles that occupied her every waking moment. She passed by the compact coffee pot, its gleaming surfaces and promise of caffeine ignored for the time being. There were no rituals tonight—only the chase.

Elle moved to her workstation, the multiple monitors flickering to life at her touch, a silent symphony of technology waking from slumber. She sank into the chair that knew the contours of her body all too well and rolled up the sleeves of her blouse, the single streak of white in her dark hair falling into her line of sight—a stark contrast she wore as a badge of authenticity.

Spread before her lay the jigsaw of the case: victim profiles, encrypted messages, and literary references that wove a sinister tapestry. She reached for the top file, fingers brushing over the grainy photo of Rebecca's smiling face—another life stolen, another puzzle piece.

"Let's see what you're trying to tell me," Elle murmured to the silent room, pulling up the digital image of Sarah's encoded message on the screen. Her hands flew over the keyboard, the bespoke algorithm she had crafted initiating its intricate dance of decryption.

As numbers and letters transformed into coherent words, Elle's focus narrowed, the world outside her screens fading away. It was here, in the heart of the code, where she found her truth, where the voices of chaos were silenced, and for a fleeting moment, the ghosts of her past stilled.

Outside, the city breathed the deep sighs of midnight, unaware of the battles fought within these walls. But inside, Agent Elle Keen waged war against the darkness, one cipher at a time.

She hesitated, frowning and glancing over her shoulder. Sometimes, she could get so obsessed with a case that she forgot the basics.

Today was no exception. She moved hastily back towards the door, realizing she'd left it unlocked.

The security footage kept playing in her mind. The figure in the footage was nearly impossible to make out. The team had already combed under the victims' cars. No tracking device. The killer cleaned up after himself. And in the footage, it had seemed as if he'd known where the cameras were, careful to evade them.

She shook her head in frustration, standing by the door motionless for a moment longer.

Then, the deadbolt clicked with a finality that echoed off the spartan walls of Elle's apartment. She paused, her hand still resting on the cool metal of the door handle, as her gaze drifted to the two picture frames perched on a nearby bookshelf. There, captured behind glass, her parents beamed back at her, their smiles undiminished by time or tragedy. Elle's chest tightened—a mixture of loss and resolve—as she took in the familiar contours of their faces; they were her silent sentinels, guardians of a legacy written in codes and ciphers.

With a sigh, she turned away from their watchful eyes and moved into the heart of her organized chaos. The ritual began, as it always did, with the soft gurgle and hiss of her coffee machine coming to life. The aroma of freshly brewed coffee soon filled the air, wrapping around her like an olfactory embrace.

Tom had told her to get some sleep. He often looked out for the more practical things in her life. But she wasn't interested in being mother henned just now. She had a penchant for staying up late, sometimes entire nights, relentlessly pursuing the corner and center pieces of a puzzle, hoping that once a single piece slotted into place, the rest of the picture would materialize.

Elle flicked on the switches to her equipment, each LED indicator springing up in a symphony of readiness. Monitors hummed quietly in anticipation, while various cables lay draped across her desk like electronic serpents, ready to strike at a moment's notice.

She shrugged off the constraints of her formal attire, peeling away the layers until she stood in the comfortable simplicity of a well-worn shirt—one that had seen more late nights and breakthroughs than any colleague at the bureau. It hung loose on her frame, a contrast to the tight grip of responsibility that constantly clung to her shoulders.

As the scent of coffee beckoned, Elle wrapped her hands around the warm mug, allowing the heat to seep into her skin. It was this routine that anchored her, that kept the tethers of the present firmly grounded amidst the specters of her past. Here, in the quiet fortitude of her solitude, she found the strength to continue her unyielding pursuit, one encrypted secret at a time.

The gaze of her parents' eyes from those photographs haunted her. They chased her to excellence. Sometimes, one needed a city on a hill they were sprinting towards.

Other times, they needed a monster to flee.

For Elle, the monster was the pain of her parents' passing.

She closed her eyes, picturing the scene. The small, red sedan wrapped around a metal barrier. Both her parents motionless. Steam rising from the hood of the crumpled vehicle.

So much blood.

She shivered.

It was incredible how a life could so dramatically change in a single instance.

Elle Keen sat at the heart of her technological web, fingers poised above the keyboard as she delved into the labyrinthine mysteries that lay scattered across her desk. The soft glow from the monitors cast angular shadows over the stacks of case files—Rebecca, Laura—each name a grim stanza in a killer's morbid poem.

She picked up Rebecca's file, her eyes scanning the cryptic symbols woven into the margins of an old letter, a haunting echo of 'Wuthering Heights.' Elle tapped a rhythm on her desk, a subconscious pattern that mirrored the cadence of the code before her. Then Laura's file—a snippet of a sonnet, its edges frayed with desperation, lines lifted from more than one work, including 'The Bell Jar.'

"Come on, think," Elle murmured to herself, connecting dots, tracing the thematic veins that ran between the victims. Her mind's eye flickered with images of dusty libraries and the crisp snap of turning pages. She aligned the references side by side, the literary threads intertwining yet not revealing their full tapestry. A pattern teased at the edge of her perception, nearly within grasp, but the final piece eluded her, slipping away like a specter in the fog of her fatigue.

"What secrets do you hold?" Elle whispered, her attention shifting to the latest victim's encoded message, a delicate puzzle begging to be solved. The algorithm she had crafted, a child of her own intellect and painstaking effort, awaited its purpose on the screen.

Her fingers danced across the keys, initiating the sequence. The algorithm unraveled the encoded message, a digital alchemist transmuting cryptic script into comprehensible language. With each line decoded, Elle leaned closer, a sculptor watching marble yield to form under the chisel's touch. It was more than a process; it was a performance where every keystroke played its part.

"Come on," she urged, her voice barely a whisper, her hair casting a shadow across her intent face. The algorithm churned, text blossoming on the screen in response to its creator's command.

"Almost there," Elle breathed, the dedication that had driven her through the ranks of the FBI now fueling her unwearying pursuit of justice. Each fragment of revealed text was another step towards understanding, a potential lifeline to prevent the next tragedy.

In the silence of her apartment, broken only by the hum of machines and the fervent tapping of keys, Elle Keen stood on the precipice of revelation, teetering on the brink of piecing together a murderer's intricate enigma.

Elle paused, her fingers hovering above the keyboard, as her gaze drifted to the photographs pinned to the wall beside her. Under the soft glow of her desk lamp, the victims' faces were lit with an ethereal light, their smiles frozen in time. Rebecca's bright eyes seemed to twinkle with unfulfilled dreams; Laura's head was cocked in a pose hinting at her once vibrant personality.

A heavy sigh escaped Elle's lips. Each woman's life had been brutally snatched away, woven into a grotesque tapestry by a killer with a perverse literary fixation. She reached out, tracing the outline of Laura's face with the tip of her finger, vowing silently to each of them that she would not rest until the monster behind their deaths was brought to justice. Their faces were more than just part of the case—they were embers stoking the fire of her resolve.

The sudden rap at the door jolted Elle from her solemn communion. Tension knitted her brow as she checked the time—past midnight. Routine and solitude were sacred here, and unexpected visitors were rare this late.

"Who is it?" Her voice was steady, betraying none of the adrenaline now coursing through her veins.

"Tom," came the muffled reply.

She unbolted the door and swung it open to reveal Agent Thomas Wright standing in the corridor, his silhouette imposing against the faint light from the hallway. His face, always so rugged, bore a deeper furrow of concern tonight.

"Hope I'm not interrupting," Tom said, his voice deep and resonant, eyes searching hers. He held up a manila envelope marked 'Evidence'. "Got something for you."

"Couldn't it wait 'til morning?" Elle couldn't mask the edge of irritation in her tone or hide the fatigue that pulled at the corners of her eyes.

"Sorry, no," he replied, stepping into the threshold but pausing as if hesitant to intrude on her sanctuary. "This can't wait. And neither can the person who keeps leaving these bodies for us to find."

Elle sighed again, stepping aside to let him in. The apartment, cluttered with the tools of her trade, was a stark contrast to Tom's clean-cut appearance. Despite the hour, he looked sharp, the blue suit hugging his muscular frame like a second skin.

"Thanks, Tom," she said, taking the envelope but avoiding his gaze, knowing it carried a silent question about her well-being.

"Elle," he began, the word hanging between them, weighted with unspoken worry.

"I'm fine," she cut in before he could finish, sealing off the conversation. It wasn't the time for personal concerns; there was work to be done, another piece of the puzzle to fit into place.

"Alright," he conceded with a nod, respecting her boundaries as always. "Just... be careful, okay? Get some rest."

"Mhmm," Elle responded, allowing herself a small smile for her partner's sake. She turned back to her desk, the fresh evidence files in hand, ready to dive back into the labyrinthine mind of a killer. As she held the folder, turning away, she realized Tom was still watching her.

She glanced back.

He looked like a forlorn puppy, waiting to be permitted to snatch the treat off his nose.

She sighed. "Wanna come in?"

Tom beamed, nodded, and stepped inside, closing the door behind him.

Elle's apartment seemed to shrink in size as Tom made his way further into the space, his broad shoulders brushing against the cluttered shelves and stacks of books. He glanced around, taking in the chaotic orderliness of Elle's domain, and couldn't help but feel a sense of awe for the way her mind worked.

"This place is a maze," he remarked, a mixture of curiosity and admiration evident in his voice.

Elle chuckled softly, her eyes twinkling with an impish glint. "Well, it helps keep my thoughts in order. Chaos on the outside, order within."

Tom nodded, appreciating the logic behind her method. He had always admired Elle's ability to find patterns where others saw only chaos. It was one of the reasons why they made such a formidable team.

He watched as she settled back at her desk, her attention fully absorbed by the contents of the envelope. The familiar intensity radiated from her as she meticulously examined each piece of evidence, piecing together fragments to form a clearer picture.

She could feel his eyes on her, and found that it didn't make her as uncomfortable as it once had.

It was a bit odd he'd stopped by in person this late at night... But again, the more practical realities of life were often lost on her when focused on a particularly intense puzzle.

Elle spread out the evidence files across her coffee table, the glossy photos and typed reports mingling with the shadows in the dim light of her living room. Tom perched on the edge of the couch, his eyes scanning the documents with a circling eagle's focus.

"What are these?" she said, tilting her head and studying the items from the manilla folder.

"Diaries," Tom said simply. "Lab finally released them. No strange prints. Only the victims'."

"Dairies?" Elle looked up. "Those weren't listed on the evidence list."

"They were," Tom said. "But belatedly. Apparently, the coroner found the diaries in the victims' pockets."

"They had their diaries on them? When they died?"

"Apparently."

Elle shifted uncomfortably. "Huh. Strange. Were they planted?"

"Don't know," Tom said with a shrug.

"Look at this," Elle pointed to a highlighted passage in one of the victim's diaries. "Rebecca wrote about her love for 'Wuthering Heights.'"

"Sarah had a battered copy of 'Romeo and Juliet' in her purse," Tom added, tapping a crime scene photo where the book lay beside the body. "Laura quoted 'The Picture of Dorian Gray' in her valedictorian speech."

"Classic literature," Elle mused, the gears turning behind her focused gaze. "It's the common thread like we've said, but I'm still not sure how it motivates the killeer."

"Maybe it's more about him than them," Tom suggested, leaning back to stretch his legs, his suit pulling taut over his sinewy frame. "Maybe he fancies himself some kind of morbid poet."

"More like a director staging his favorite scenes," Elle replied, a wry smile momentarily brightening her features. "Only the actors don't get up after the curtain call."

"Macabre theater," Tom quipped, but his smirk faded as he caught Elle's steely expression. She was back in the depths, her mind weaving through the darkness they sought to illuminate.

Elle sifted through the photographs, her fingertips brushing over the victims' faces. "These women were chosen for a reason," she said, her voice low, haunted by the gravity of their lost lives.

"Staging literary deaths... it's theatrical, obsessive." Tom leaned forward, elbows on knees, the poppy above his lapel catching the light as he glanced over at Elle. "Our guy is putting on a show, but why? What's he trying to say?"

"Or who he's trying to impress." Elle's brow furrowed as she considered the possibility. "Each scene is meticulously planned, like he's recreating the stories that obsessed him."

"An audience of one, maybe." Tom's gaze hardened. "Someone who understands his twisted narrative."

"Or an attempt to rewrite his own story," Elle offered, her voice tinged with empathy for the minds she worked so tirelessly to decode. "Either way, we're dealing with someone who finds solace in the dramatic finality of these tales."

"Solace and power," Tom agreed, nodding grimly. "He controls how the story ends for each of them."

Silence settled over them, thick with unspoken thoughts. They were partners, yes, bound by duty and a shared resolve. But in moments like these, they were also kindred spirits, united in their fight against the encroaching darkness, each driven by their own demons and desires to see justice served.

The shrill ring of Elle's phone shattered the contemplative silence. Fingers that had been tracing the grim futures of victims now fumbled urgently for the vibrating device, its glow a harsh intrusion in the dimly lit room. Tom watched, his eyes narrowing as the color drained from her face with each sharp trill.

The office was calling. No, dispatch. Shit. This late at night?

Elle felt a cold hand tightening around her heart. There was really only one reason for a call this late... Double shit.

"Keen," she answered, her voice betraying none of the dread that tightened its grip around her heart. She listened; the line crackled with static and urgency, the words on the other end punctuating the stillness with stark clarity.

"Another one?" Her hand clenched involuntarily, knuckles whitening as the phone became an anchor to the grim reality. There was a beat of silence so profound it felt like the world held its breath – then she was on her feet, the chair screeching a protest against the sudden movement.

"On our way," she said simply, then hung up.

Tom was already standing, staring at her, eyes the size of quarters. "No good?" he said.

"Another."

"Shit."

"Info?"

"Some. Not much."

"What do we know?"

"A woman named Sarah Mason," she whispered, her eyes locked with Tom's, conveying volumes in a look. "She... she’s staged. Poison." The words tumbled out, heavy with a significance that hung palpably in the air between them.

"Damn it." The expletive was a growl, torn from Tom's chest. He raked a hand through his hair, the frustration and anger palpable.

The killer's game—a perverse homage to literature's darkest moments—was far from over. Each victim was a chapter, each crime scene a stanza in a morbid poem they were racing to interpret. And Sarah Mason, a name now etched in loss, was the latest verse in this macabre narrative.

"Let's go," Elle said, her voice steeling as she grabbed her jacket. She couldn't afford the luxury of grief—not yet.

Tom followed suit, his movements precise, efficient. They were partners, cast into the night with the weight of a new name on their conscience, and the unyielding resolve to rewrite the ending of a killer's deranged script.

CHAPTER TWELVE

The crime scene was fitting to the crime and chosen for the obvious overtones.

The worn soles of Elle's shoes slapped against the cold, polished floor as she and Tom hastened through the yawning maw of the local theater's double doors. The once welcoming space now stretched before them, cavernous and hushed in the dead of night, the kind of quiet that presses in on the ears, thick with anticipation and dread.

"Keep your eyes open," she muttered, her voice barely above a whisper, though there was no one around to overhear. Her pulse thrummed a staccato rhythm against her temples, each beat a reminder of what awaited them on stage.

Tom gave a curt nod, his jaw set firm. His eyes, dark pools reflecting the sparse overhead lighting, scanned the expanse. They moved in a practiced cadence, side by side yet each alone with their thoughts, their steps synchronized even in urgency.

Elle felt the emptiness of the auditorium envelop them. Rows upon rows of plush red seats fanned out like specters of an unseen audience, the silence so palpable it seemed a character unto itself. It was a stark contrast to the usual bustle and hum of life that theaters breathed—a place where stories unfolded and emotions ran high. Now, all that remained was the echo of absence.

As they approached the edge of the stage, a chill skittered down Elle's spine. Here, under the harsh glare of the spotlights, the stage was prepped for its final act, a grim tableau waiting for them. She could feel the weight of the tragedy that had unfolded here, the stillness of the air like a held breath before the plunge into chaos.

"Ready?" Tom's voice was steady, but his hand hovered near the service weapon at his hip, an unconscious testament to the unease that gripped them both.

"Not really," Elle replied, her gaze fixed on the silent stage. There were answers hidden within the eerie tranquility, and she would unearth them, cipher by cipher, until the truth broke free from its cryptic bonds.

Together, they stepped onto the stage, and the reality of what lay before them began to unfurl.

Three cops lingered off to the wings, watching from where crime scene tape was being stretched over an exit.

She nodded towards the first responders, a brief tempo of gratitude in the dark stillness. What time was it?

Her stifled yawn hinted at the late hour.

Elle's shoes made a soft thud against the wooden planks of the stage, the sound oddly muffled in the vast emptiness of the theater. The spotlight carved out an island of stark brightness in the otherwise dim space, and within that harsh circle of light lay the body of Sarah.

"Another one," Elle whispered, her voice barely louder than the silence enveloping them. It was as though the very air had been sucked out of the room, leaving behind only the ghostly echo of applause that would never come again.

She crouched beside the staged death scene, her keen eyes scanning the macabre setting. It was meticulously arranged, each prop placed with purposeful precision. The killer had transformed this space into his canvas, and the tragedy that unfolded upon it was his perverse masterpiece.

Tom paced along the edge of the stage, stepping carefully to avoid disturbing any potential evidence. "It's like he's taunting us," he muttered, shaking his head in disbelief.

"Or inviting us to understand," Elle countered, her mind already sifting through the visual cues before her. She noted the position of the body, the arrangement of the surrounding items—a spilled vial, a crumpled letter—each object a potential key to unlocking the motivations of their enigmatic adversary.

The crime scene's eerie silence seemed to press against her eardrums, yet within that quietude, she could almost hear the whisper of code strings rearranging themselves, forming patterns that called out for decryption. To others, the stillness might have been unnerving, but to Elle, it was a blank slate on which the truth awaited inscription.

Every prop felt significant, every mark deliberate. A wilted rose here, a torn piece of fabric there; it was as if the killer had left breadcrumbs, a trail that only someone with Elle's unique blend of talent and tenacity could follow.

"Look at this," Tom said, gesturing towards a seemingly innocuous scuff mark on the stage floor near the body. Elle approached, kneeling down to inspect the irregularity more closely. Her fingers hovered above it, careful not to disturb the delicate narrative being woven by this morbid display.

"Every detail is intentional," she murmured, her brain cataloging the scene, filing away each observation for later analysis. "We're dealing with someone who sees death as an art form, and these... are his exhibits."

"Disturbing thought," Tom replied, his expression grim.

"Truth often is," Elle replied, her gaze still locked onto the scattered clues before her. There was a message here, hidden amidst the theatrics, and Elle Keen would decipher it.

Elle's footsteps were silent on the stage, a stark contrast to the scream of silence that enveloped the theater. Her eyes scanned the macabre tableau before her, and she paused, a cold realization washing over her. The lifeless body of Sarah, arrayed in an ancient gown, lay with one hand resting over her heart, the other clutching an empty vial. An ornate dagger was positioned just out of reach, its blade catching the ghostly light.

"Tom," Elle called softly, her voice steady despite the chill that crept up her spine. "It's Juliet. Sarah is Juliet."

Tom stepped closer, his brows knitting together as he took in the scene. "Juliet?"

"From Shakespeare's play. Her death... it's been staged to mirror Juliet's suicide." Elle's analytical mind raced, piecing together the significances and implications.

"Romeo and Juliet," Tom muttered, understanding dawning in his eyes.

"Exactly. He's obsessed," Elle confirmed, her gaze never leaving the morose display.

She edged closer to the body, her keen eyes sweeping over every element of the setup. There, amidst the props—a crumpled page. Elle crouched, using tweezers to pick up the paper delicately. The text was familiar, the words from 'Romeo and Juliet', but upon closer examination, Elle noticed irregularities—words crossed out, others written over with meticulous care.

"Another coded message," she whispered, her pulse quickening with the thrill of the challenge. She held the page aloft for Tom to see. "Our killer left us another puzzle to solve."

"Can you make anything out?" Tom asked, peering at the page from over her shoulder.

"Not yet," Elle said, her mind already working through possible decryption strategies. Codes were a comfort, a language she understood better than any spoken word. They were finite, solvable. Crimes like these, woven with human madness and cruelty, were messier, but the code provided an anchor, a way in.

"Let's bag it and get it back to the lab. You're the best shot we have at cracking this," Tom suggested, his confidence in her abilities a warmth and support despite the frigidity now gripping her bones.

Elle nodded, carefully sliding the page into an evidence bag. A puzzle within a tragedy, a cipher wrapped in a sonnet of death—this was the world Elle navigated best.

Elle's fingers hovered over her digital recorder, the red light blinking steadily in the dim stage lighting. "Documenting additional evidence," she stated, a clinical lilt to her words as she described the page from 'Romeo and Juliet.' She detailed each aberrant mark, each overwritten word with meticulous precision, knowing the recording would be vital when she later tackled the decryption.

"Serial number on the paper corresponds to the edition found at the first crime scene," she continued, her brain already sifting through cryptographic techniques that might peel away the layers of the killer's message.

"It does?" Tom said, glancing sharply at her.

"Yes. On the second shelf. Fourth book from the left," she rattled off, picturing the crime scene in her mind.

Tom nodded, impressed.

She'd often taken her skill with memory for granted, but sometimes, she was reminded that not everyone's mind worked the same way. In part, she'd been born with a gift. Nothing more than that. It didn't make her better than anyone. Didn't mean she mattered more. All it meant was that she had a responsibility towards others to help them with her gift.

But also, her parents had trained her. Had brought her up as a puzzle-solving machine. To be someone who *could* be of use to others.

This was only more responsibility. Sometimes, the weight of feeling as if she *owed* others was a crushing burden. And even now, she could feel it pressing down on her, threatening to smother her.

She took in a slow, steadying breath.

As she stood on the stage, by the crime scene, her keen eyes caught a glint near the edge of the stage—a remnant waiting to be noticed. Elle reached for an evidence bag, then gingerly picked up the fragments of an antique fountain pen, its nib stained with dried ink. Her thoughts pivoted swiftly; could this be the same writing instrument used to alter the text? Or perhaps it was a deliberate plant, a clue intended to mislead or signal?

She recited into her recording device, "Antique fountain pen components found approximately five meters from the body. Possible connection to Emma Wilson—known collector—or unidentified suspect." She sealed the evidence with a satisfying snap.

With the clues secured, Elle's gaze swept across the stage, where Tom and the forensic team were huddled over Sarah's body. The analysts worked with quiet efficiency, their movements practiced and respectful, while Tom offered a steady presence, his scarred face set in concentration. He glanced up, catching Elle's eye for a moment, offering a nod of silent solidarity before returning to the grim task.

Elle shifted her attention back to the stage, where chaos reigned in the form of scattered props and dramatic lighting. The bloodstains on the wooden floorboards seemed to mar the very soul of the theater, but to Elle, they were coordinates in a grander design, pieces of a larger puzzle only she could solve.

She moved methodically, absorbing every detail. A torn piece of fabric here, the angle of a fallen chair there—all potential indicators of the killer's movements and methods. Elle traced her hands along the scenery backdrops, feeling for anomalies, her fingertips brushing against textures, cataloging each new sensation.

To others, the stage might have appeared as a mere setting of macabre theatrics, but Elle's mind reconstructed the narrative hidden within the disarray. Every misplaced prop felt like a deliberate choice, a breadcrumb left behind by a twisted mind. And Elle, with her unique perception of order within pandemonium, would follow the trail wherever it led.

"Patterns," she murmured to herself, her voice barely audible over the hum of activity around her. "There are always patterns." She took another step, her eyes never ceasing their hunt, her determination etched into every line of her focused expression. This stage was her arena now, and she would not rest until every secret was laid bare.

Elle lingered at the edge of the stage, her gaze entrenched in the macabre scene before her. The stark contrast of the victim's pallor against the scarlet drapery snagged her thoughts, a morbid canvas that beckoned with a silent scream for interpretation. All at once, it clicked—a revelation piercing through the fog of method and motive.

"Tom," she called out, her voice steady despite the tumult churning within her. He looked up from his meticulous note-taking beside the forensics team, his dark eyes locking onto hers.

"Artwork," she stated, stepping closer to him. "He's an artist. A sick one." Her hand swept across the air, framing the scene. "This isn't just about killing. It's about creating—each murder a twisted masterpiece."

Tom straightened, the lines of his scarred face hardening as if the truth had carved itself into his features. "Literary deaths..." he murmured, connecting the dots. "You think he's using them as inspiration?"

"More than that," Elle insisted, her mind racing with the implications. "He's staging them meticulously, every death a reenactment of literature's most tragic ends. It's his signature, his exhibition."

"Yes... we know that already, though. Don't we?"

"No, don't you see? This is more... it's... it's his work. He's not doing this for vengeance, but for beauty. This is his version of beauty. This is his art. His life's work. His masterpiece."

It all was clicking into place now. "Which means, he *wants* to be found. No artist wants to live in obscurity.

She glanced towards the evidence baggie with the altered literature page. "Each scene had those coded pages... He wants to be discovered. he wants his name known," she rattled off, feeling a rising sense of excitement. "That means we can find him, Tom, don't you see?"

"Then we might predict his next move," Tom suggested, catching on. "If we can pinpoint which literary death he's likely to replicate..."

"Exactly." Elle's eyes were alight with the flames of deduction. "We need to dive into the classics, any work that glorified death in its prose. We profile the killer through his art, and we anticipate his next creation."

"Risky," Tom said, but his tone carried a note of respect. "But damn if it doesn't make sense."

"Riskier still is to wait for another body to drop," Elle countered, her resolve unwavering. "We have to get ahead of his narrative."

Tom nodded, the weight of their task settling over them. Together, they turned back toward the grotesque diorama, their minds weaving through the annals of literature, seeking the thread that would lead them to a killer who penned death in the ink of life's final breath.

Elle's boots clicked against the theater's side stage, the sound an eerie punctuation to the night's grim cadence. The scent of dust and lingering perfume from Sarah's last performance hung in the air like a morbid backdrop. She cast a final glance over her shoulder at the macabre scene, the stark lighting casting long shadows across the stage where life had imitated art far too closely.

"Third victim," she whispered to herself, weaving through the tangle of police tape as if it were cobwebs. The thought writhed in her mind, urgent and insistent. The killer was out there, perhaps watching, plotting the next chapter in his deranged narrative. Elle felt the familiar itch at the base of her skull, the one that signaled her brain was piecing together puzzles no one else could see.

She paused at the edge of the stage, hand brushing against the cool metal frame. The analytical gears in her mind whirred, processing every shred of evidence, every whispered word of the past hours. Her parents had taught her that knowledge was not just power—it was armor, and in this moment, her intellect was the shield against the chaos that threatened to engulf her.

"Keen!" called Tom from behind her, his voice pulling her back to the present. She didn't look back. There was no need; his presence was a steadfast constant, even when the world seemed to spiral into madness.

"Got it," she called back, more to herself than him. She was already moving, each step away from the carnage a step closer to prevention, to salvation. She could almost see the threads of the killer's plan unwinding before her, a sinister tapestry of death and prose.

As she emerged from the dark maw of the theater, the night air hit her face, cool and sharp. It jolted her senses, reaffirming the reality of the hunt. She felt it then—a spark igniting within, the kindled fire of a challenge met with equal force. Her mind was a weapon, honed by years of loss and triumph, and it thrummed with the energy of the chase.

The streetlights flickered overhead, casting pools of light that danced over her dark, walnut hair and the singular white streak that marked her history. Elle didn't bother to shield her eyes from the glare. She saw clearly, more clearly than ever—the path ahead, the work to be done, the lives to be saved.

He wanted to be found. And she was determined to oblige him.

As she stood in the dark street, she hesitated, frowning and glancing around.

Could he resist watching them? Resist witnessing the first reaction to his life's work?

She paused, scanning windows and alleyways, looking for cameras.

For a moment, a slow chill crept down her spine, and she wondered if she was being watched.

CHAPTER THIRTEEN

A restless night had turned to a few hours of sleep and then more than a natural portion of caffeine.

Now, the fuel from the aforementioned caffeine propelled Elle Keen up the sidewalk, towards the cafe where she'd agreed to meet with her partner.

The victim last night had given her a new certainty. The killer wasn't just a killer. In fact, it might not even have been his primary motive. Death was a means to an end.

His *art,* as he saw it, was the core goal. This gave them new parameters. It was a small tweak to the profile they'd been operating under, but a crucial one.

Elle pushed open the door to the quaint coffee shop, the aroma of roasted beans and the quiet hum of indie folk music welcoming her inside. Her sharp gaze immediately found Tom; he was hard to miss, commanding the small space with his presence even as he sat hunched over his laptop, fingers tapping a syncopated rhythm on the keys. The tailored lines of his blue suit appeared almost sculptural against the backdrop of the worn leather chair he occupied, a silent testament to the coiled strength beneath.

As she approached, Elle's mind whirled with the urgency that had propelled them into this haven of caffeine and pastries. Their current case was a labyrinth of literary allusions, each crime scene a grotesque homage to the classics. Elle's thoughts were a jumble of quotes and motifs from "Romeo and Juliet" and "The Picture of Dorian Gray" combined with an array of Shakespeare's other works. It was as if the killer was using the pages of these storied texts as a blueprint for their macabre masterpieces. The intensity of their search was not just about catching a murderer; it felt personal to Elle, almost as if each clue deciphered was a step toward vindicating her parents' untimely deaths.

"Find anything?" she asked, pulling out the chair opposite Tom, her voice cutting through the cozy ambiance of the shop.

Tom glanced up, his dark eyes reflecting a fervor matching her own. "It's like trying to piece together a puzzle where you don't even know what the final picture looks like," he said, a hint of frustration lacing his tone. "But there has to be a pattern. The way 'Romeo and Juliet' speaks of star-crossed lovers and death—it's too specific to our scenes to be coincidence."

"Right," Elle agreed, her fingers already itching to fly across her own keyboard. "And 'Dorian Gray,' with its themes of superficiality and the corruption of the soul... This killer is not just leaving bodies. It's more about *them* than the victims. That was our initial mistake."

She glanced at Tom, mildly impressed, but also somewhat irritated that he'd arrived before her.

She prided herself on working longer hours, staying up later and waking up earlier than her colleagues, but Tom Wright was no slouch. Still, she made a mental note to set her alarm for an hour earlier next time they met up at this familiar hot spot.

She sat at the table, pulling out a chair and swinging her laptop bag's strap from off her shoulder.

"Black," Tom said. "No sugar." He nodded towards the steaming mug set in front of her. "Not sure how you drink that swill... but it's your oder at least."

She nodded in gratitude, and glanced towards Tom's own drink, which looked like a milkshake with the amount of sugar and cream he placed into it.

Tom's eyes flickered to the barista behind the counter, a young woman with a bright smile and an alluring aura. Elle followed his gaze and couldn't help but roll her eyes. It seemed that wherever they went, women were drawn to Tom like moths to a flame. He had a charm that was hard to resist, even if he didn't intentionally wield it.

The barista was mouthing something to Tom, wiggling her eyebrows. And he returned the attention.

"Focus, Tom," Elle said, snapping her laptop open. "We're on a tight schedule here."

He chuckled, a deep rumble that vibrated through the air. "Oh come on, Elle. Can't blame a guy for enjoying some friendly conversation."

Elle pretended not to hear his teasing remark as she navigated her way through various search engines and databases, trying to find any connection between the works of literature and their potential suspects. Her fingers flew across the keyboard, her mind working ten steps ahead.

Tom's eagerness to fuel their marathon session was palpable as he flagged down the waitress with a genial lift of his hand. "Two of your strongest coffees, please. Extra shots if you can manage it," he ordered, his voice carrying the unmistakable timbre of resolve.

"Coming right up," the waitress chirped, tucking a loose strand of hair behind her ear as she offered him a smile that seemed to stretch just a fraction wider than necessary. She lingered, her gaze tracing the rugged landscape of his scarred face and the military precision of his crew cut.

"Make sure it's strong enough to wake the dead," Tom added, flashing a roguish grin that seemed to belong in a different era, one of black-and-white film and sharp-tongued detectives.

Elle noted the exchange with an internal eye-roll, but refused to let the flirtation distract her from the task at hand. Her mind was a whirlwind of Shakespearean quotes and Wildean paradoxes, each potentially a vital clue to understanding the twisted psyche they were chasing. Elle's fingers poised over the keys, ready to dissect digital archives and databases with the same meticulous scrutiny she applied to every coded mystery since childhood.

"Will do," the waitress replied, casting a final, playful glance at Tom before she sashayed away. Elle could almost hear the silent exchange of unspoken promises and light-hearted banter, the kind that never failed to spark brief irritation within her. She did not have time for such trivialities—not when there were patterns to be found and lives hanging in the balance.

"Focus, Keen," she muttered under her breath, tuning out the ambient hum of the coffee shop and the low murmur of conversations around them. The taste of Chinese food from last night's takeout still lingered faintly on her tongue, a reminder of simpler pleasures. But now, her appetite was purely for the truth; she hungered for the breakthrough that would lead them to the killer, and she would devour every byte of information until it revealed itself.

Elle's eyes flickered across the screen, the blue light casting a ghostly hue on her determined features. Her mind churned through pages of information with the same precision that had once unraveled the most complex of codes in her youth. Now, amidst an array of open tabs, she sought connections within the literary labyrinths of 'Romeo and Juliet' and 'The Picture of Dorian Gray', hunting for the intellectual thread that tied these works to the grisly murders.

"Anything yet?" Tom's voice pierced her concentration, his eagerness a sharp contrast to the silence of her internal calculations.

"Still digging," Elle replied, her words terse as she brushed a lock of walnut hair streaked with premature white from her face. She could feel the weight of urgency pressing upon her shoulders, a heaviness matched only by the ticking clock of an unsub growing bolder with each passing day.

Her fingers danced over the keys, diving into forums discussing Shakespeare's use of death as a character, scouring art critics' interpretations of Dorian Gray's descent into madness. But the digital landscape was sprawling and unwieldy, offering no immediate gifts of revelation. Each click, each search seemed to lead further into an abyss of conjecture and dead ends.

The point was the killer. It was about him. A narcissist. It wasn't as much about his victims.

That was the new revelation she was operating under.

After taking another sip of her coffee, Elle focused her attention on the screen in front of her. She began typing furiously, scouring the internet in search of anyone who might've had a connection to literature and art. Anything that stood out, especially among local talent. Anyone who styled themselves something of a creator. It was a tedious task, but she knew that if they could find a pattern, they might be able to predict the killer's next move.

Minutes turned into hours as the two of them delved deeper into their research. The coffee shop grew louder with the chatter of patrons around them, but Elle barely noticed. Her mind was consumed by the words on the screen—blogs, articles, social media posts—all potential leads to unravel this twisted puzzle.

Tom ordered a couple more extra-strength coffees, each one with an added shot of caffeine. He asked the waitress what drink had the most caffeine and ordered two of them, determined to keep up with Elle's relentless pace. As he carried the steaming cups back to their table, Elle couldn't help but notice the flirty glances exchanged between the waitress and her partner. He flashed his charismatic smile in return, his natural charm effortlessly drawing people towards him.

Elle's annoyance rose as she observed this interaction. She had always prided herself on her focus and determination, and yet here was Tom charming his way through conversations without even trying. It frustrated her in a way she couldn't quite explain—perhaps a mix of jealousy and irritation at his apparent ease with people.

But she quickly pushed aside her growing irritation and refocused on her work. Her eyes scanned through a blog post that referenced Juliet's suicide. She frowned at the comments beneath the blog, and clicked the link to the commentor's own posts.

Nothing... The page was empty. She grits her teeth.

The frustration simmered within her, a familiar heat that threatened to boil over with each fruitless attempt to connect the dots. A string of code, a pattern in prose—anything that could point them toward the next victim before it was too late. It was like grappling with shadows.

"Come on," she whispered to herself, a silent plea to the universe, to the very fibers of the web that entrapped them. "Give me something." The cursor blinked mockingly, a solitary sentinel amidst a sea of unyielding data.

"Deep breaths, Elle," Tom murmured from across the table, sensing her mounting tension. "We'll crack this." He downed another glass full of cream and sugar with a smidge of coffee.

She exhaled slowly, forcing her mind to reset to approach the problem from a new angle. There had to be a clue lurking somewhere within the chaos, a breadcrumb left by a killer who taunted them with theatrical displays of violence and artistry. But where?

In that moment, with the coffee shop around her fading into a blurred backdrop, Elle felt the razor-sharp edge of desperation—a need for clarity that cut deeper than any craving for comfort or companionship. The breakthrough was out there, hidden within the lines of text scrolling past her vision. And she would find it, by sheer force of will if necessary.

Tom pushed back from the table and flagged down the waitress again, a wisp of his military-style discipline evident in the gesture. Elle watched him from the corner of her eye, not wanting to divert too much attention from her screen, where coded messages danced just beyond comprehension.

"Excuse me," he said, voice smooth but commanding. "Mind if we stay here a bit longer? Other tables are open."

"Sure!" she said excitedly. "By the way, I asked the manager for our strongest drink. You're looking for the Eye-Opener Special. Double shot of espresso with a drip coffee chaser. It's like getting a caffeine IV."

"Perfect. Two of those, please."

As the waitress scribbled on her notepad, Elle's focus momentarily faltered. The soft hum of the coffee machine, the clink of ceramic, and the low rumble of conversation around them all faded into a hazy background. A pang, sharp and unexpected, tightened in her chest as she saw the waitress slip a folded piece of paper toward Tom. It was casual, almost imperceptible, but it was enough. Enough to stir the green-eyed monster lurking beneath Elle's composed exterior.

The waitress hurried away to fulfill the order as Tom tucked the paper smoothly into his wallet. She caught a glimpse of a phone number.

"Looks like you made quite the impression," Elle remarked dryly, her words laced with unintended edge as she met Tom's gaze.

He glanced down at the number, a flicker of surprise in his dark eyes before he slid it into his pocket without missing a beat. "Just part of the job," he quipped, though his tone held a note of satisfaction. "Gathering intel comes in many forms."

"Right. Intel." Elle turned back to her laptop, her fingers resuming their rapid dance across the keys. She delved back into the search, the familiar grid of data offering a refuge from the irritation that pricked at her. But even as she tunneled deeper into the digital labyrinth, the image of that discreet exchange lurked at the edges of her consciousness, unwelcome and persistent.

Elle's eyes darted across the screen, the soft glow of her laptop casting shadows on her intent face. The clatter of keys against the tabletop was a persistent rhythm against the muted ambiance of the coffee shop. She filtered through countless tabs, the works of Shakespeare and Wilde splayed in endless digital threads before her.

And then, a flicker of something new caught her attention—a blog post etched in gothic font, touting an intimate familiarity with the darker side of human nature. Elle leaned closer, her pulse quickening. The name Robert Brown headlined the page, accompanied by a stark black-and-white photo of a man with piercing eyes.

She'd searched for the blog name of the man who'd commented on the initial post. He'd started a different blog, and this one was well-populated with posts ranging back almost a decade.

She could read the hyperlinked dates on the sidebar, and

each led to a chilling exploration of death, despair, and the twisted depths of the human psyche. Robert Brown seemed to revel in the macabre, his words dripping with a disturbing fascination for tragedy and suffering.

Elle's heart quickened as she scrolled through the blog, her mind racing to connect the dots between Robert Brown's sinister online presence and the murders they were investigating. The more she read, the more convinced she became that this wasn't just a normal online poster.

"Tom," she said, her voice barely above a whisper, her eyes never leaving the screen. "I think we found our guy."

Tom's chair scraped against the floor as he stood up, his curiosity piqued by Elle's urgency. "What did you find?"

"It's Robert Brown," Elle replied, her voice laced with a mix of excitement and unease. She turned the laptop towards him, her finger pointing at the screen. "Look at these blog posts. They're filled with darkness, obsession with death, and references to Shakespearean tragedies."

Tom leaned closer, scanning the screen intently. "This is definitely suspicious," he said, furrowing his brow. "But we need more than just a blog to make an arrest."

"I know," Elle admitted. "But we can't ignore this connection. We need to gather more evidence."

"Alright... so who is this guy exactly. Robert... wait, what did you say his name was?"

"Robert Brown," she began, scrolling through the blog entries. "Local theater director. He's recently put on performances of 'Romeo and Juliet' and 'The Picture of Dorian Gray.'"

"Classics," Tom mused. "Same as our victims. Shit. But what's the catch?"

"Listen to this," Elle continued, her fingers pausing as she read aloud from the screen. "'Death is not an end but a transformation; the ultimate act in the theater of life.'" Her voice took on a chilling cadence as she echoed Brown's words. "His posts are littered with similar musings—a dark fascination with the macabre."

"Any direct mentions of the murders?" Tom asked, his brow furrowed.

"Not explicitly," Elle replied, "but the subtext—it's eerie how much it aligns with our cases. And look here—complaints filed against him for abusive practices during rehearsals. Actors pushed to their mental limits for the sake of 'authenticity.'"

"Could be our guy," Tom nodded, his own eyes narrowing as he processed the information. "He's using art to justify obsession... maybe even murder."

"Or he's a red herring," Elle countered, her analytical mind churning. "But we can't ignore the coincidence. Not with stakes this high."

"Agreed." Tom's hand reached out, hovering over the mouse pad. "Let's dig deeper into this Robert Brown."

Together, they plunged back into the depths of the web, the hunt for truth propelling them forward as the afternoon light waned outside the refuge of the small coffee shop.

Elle tapped her phone, the screen illuminating her face with a cold glow as she dialed the local precinct's number. The coffee shop's ambient noise receded into the background as she focused on the task at hand.

"Detective Morris, please," she said when the call connected, her tone clipped and professional. She glanced at Tom, who watched her with an unwavering gaze, his scarred face betraying nothing of the tension they both felt.

"Speaking," came the gruff response from the other end.

"Agent Keen, FBI. We're following up on a Robert Brown associated with recent performances at the local theater—"

"Ah, Brown," Morris cut in, a note of recognition in his voice. "We've had our eyes on him. A few run-ins for disturbing behavior. Nothing stuck but ruffled feathers and bad reviews."

"Any connections to the victims?" Elle asked, her mind racing through possibilities.

"Which case is this again, Agent Keen?"

"The classics-inspired murders," Elle clarified, her voice steady. "The victims have all been found in tableaus that mirror scenes from Romeo and Juliet and The Picture of Dorian Gray."

There was a brief pause on the other end of the line, followed by a sigh. "I can't say for sure, but there's definitely some overlap. Brown's productions centered around those plays, and some of his former actors have complained about his obsession with authenticity."

"So people have filed reports?"

"That's right. Nothing particularly actionable. Mostly mean words... Long hours. Nothing that could be proved. Nothing concrete. But given your interest... I'd say it's worth a second look." Morris sounded wary now, cautious not to dismiss their hunch.

"Thank you, Detective. We'll be in touch," Elle said before ending the call. She met Tom's intent stare. "PD's had issues with him, too. No direct ties to the victims, but it's enough to warrant a closer inspection."

"Then let's not waste any more time here," Tom declared, pushing back his chair with a scrape against the floor.

As they gathered their things, Elle couldn't help but notice the small piece of paper with scribbled digits that lay beside Tom's laptop—a memento from the flirtatious waitress. Evidently, he'd taken it out of his pocket to study the digits. She quirked an eyebrow, her lips curving in a smirk.

"Planning on calling for a late-night caffeine fix or something more, Agent Wright?" Her voice held a teasing edge, a rare moment of levity between the intensity of their work.

Tom pocketed the number with a roguish grin. "Strictly professional curiosity," he quipped, though his dark eyes flickered with amusement.

"Of course," Elle replied, her tone dry. "Because we can't have too much 'professional curiosity' during an investigation."

They stepped out of the coffee shop into the fading daylight, leaving behind the scent of roasted beans and the low hum of conversations. The morning air was cool and crisp, carrying with it the promise of autumn and the unknowns of their impending encounter.

"Ready to meet this theatrical mastermind?" Tom asked as they made their way down the sidewalk towards the parking lot, his stride confident and purposeful.

"Let's just hope this isn't another act in his drama," Elle responded, her mind already sifting through strategies for their confrontation with Robert Brown.

CHAPTER FOURTEEN

Elle felt a cold tendril wrap around her heart--the dread of arriving too late. The director's posts were darker and darker still the more she read them.

She frowned from where she sat in the passenger seat, reading a post titled *Ode to the Grim.*

In the dim glow of the car's interior, Elle's eyes scanned the screen of her laptop, her brows furrowing with growing concern. The post she was reading, titled "Ode to the Grim," sent a chill down her spine. The words dripped with an unsettling obsession for death and darkness, as if the author was intoxicated by the very concept he wrote about.

"Tom," she spoke, her voice edged with urgency, "this post...it's disturbing. Robert Brown seems fixated on morbidity and suffering."

Tom glanced at her briefly, his eyes narrowing in response to her tone. "What did you find?"

Elle angled the screen towards him, tracing her finger along the lines of the blog post. "He talks about how pain and despair are the true essence of art. It's almost as if he revels in suffering."

Tom's grip on the steering wheel tightened, his knuckles turning white. "That doesn't bode well. We need to find him now. His theater is just up ahead."

The industrial skeleton of the warehouse loomed before them like a forgotten mausoleum, its rusted exterior walls a testament to years of neglect.

They parked and hastily exited the vehicle. Elle felt the gravitas of the place seep into her bones as she and Tom approached the large metal door hanging askew on its hinges. It squealed open with a protest that echoed through the cavernous space within, like an unwelcome guest at a funeral.

"Charming place," Tom muttered under his breath, his eyes scanning the shadows for any sign of movement. He adjusted the cuff of his tailored blue suit, the fabric whispering against his skin—a juxtaposition of order against the chaotic entropy of their surroundings.

"Looks like something straight out of a gothic novel," Elle replied, her voice low and even. Her gaze followed the contours of the decrepit structure, every corner and crevice potentially hiding more than just dust and decay.

Robert Brown, the man they were here to confront, had chosen an appropriate lair for his peculiar brand of theatrics. The vast emptiness of the warehouse hinted at the grand visions that must have once played out in this space, now only haunting memories etched into the cold concrete floor.

"Robert has a flair for the dramatic," Elle continued, her mind piecing together the man's reputation with what lay before her. "But there's a fine line between genius and madness, and I have a feeling we're about to find out which side of it he sits on."

Tom nodded, his dark eyes sharp with the anticipation of the unknown. "Let's just hope he's willing to talk before putting on a show."

They stepped further into the dimness, the silence around them thickening. To Elle, who preferred the clear-cut world of codes and ciphers, the unpredictability of human behavior often proved to be the most complex puzzle. She tightened her grip on her firearm, ready for whatever act was about to unfold.

Elle's boot crunched on a scatter of sawdust as she stepped further into the cavernous space. Shadows loomed like specters above half-constructed stage sets, their skeletal frameworks veiled in cobwebs. The air was stale, heavy with the scent of damp wood and rusting metal. Strewn across the concrete floor lay a smattering of abandoned props—a chipped porcelain mask, a dulled rapier, and countless scripts with curled edges, each a silent testament to the frenzied mind that had brought them into existence.

"Chaos," Elle murmured, her eyes scanning the disarray. "An organized mind wouldn't leave his thoughts so... scattered."

Tom grunted in agreement, stepping over a toppled Corinthian column that looked as if it had been part of a set for some ancient tragedy. The disorder spoke volumes about Robert Brown—the brilliant yet controversial theater director they were here to question. It was a physical echo of the tumultuous reputation that swirled around him, brilliance teetering on the brink of madness.

They advanced cautiously between the debris, the faint light from the high windows casting elongated shadows that danced with their movements. Elle noted every detail, her trained eye deciphering this chaotic sketch as if it were one of her beloved puzzles. Here, a stack of weathered books on the grotesque—there, a collection of twisted sculptures that could only have sprung from a disturbed imagination.

"Robert Brown?" Tom called out, his voice firm yet non-threatening.

A sudden clatter echoed from the far end of the warehouse as a figure emerged from the darkness. With a start, Elle registered the wild hair, the intense eyes, and the taut lines of a body wound up tight as a coiled spring. It was Robert, no doubt.

"Who dares?" he barked, his voice echoing off the high ceiling, loaded with a hostility that jarred against the quietude of the place.

Elle's hand instinctively went to her weapon, though she kept it holstered. Her pulse quickened. This was not the controlled confrontation she had hoped for. Every nerve ending pricked with heightened alertness, and the warning bells in her mind clanged with urgency. Something about Robert's immediate aggression was off—it wasn't merely defensive, it was frantic, erratic.

"FBI, sir. Mr. Brown, we just want to talk," Elle said, her tone even but clear. She stood her ground, watching as Robert's gaze flickered with something akin to desperation. His stance was aggressive, but his eyes betrayed a fear that didn't quite fit the image of a man confident in his innocence.

"Talk?" Robert spat the word as if it burned his tongue. "You come into my sanctuary with talk of treachery and expect me to simper and bow? I know your kind!"

Elle took a careful step forward, her mind racing to decode this new variable. She had expected resistance, perhaps even evasion—but outright hostility? That was an anomaly she hadn't anticipated. And anomalies, in Elle's world, were clues that begged to be understood.

Robert's eyes, wild with an unvoiced terror, darted from Elle to Tom and back again, like a cornered animal calculating its chances.

He reached over, and his hand grasped the hilt of a prop rapier. "En guarde, sir!" Robert screamed. Then, with a visceral yell that echoed off the walls of the warehouse, he lunged forward, not at Elle, but at Tom, rapier held high.

Tom cursed. Elle's gun leapt up, but no clear shot. Tom was in the way.

Tom's reflexes were lightning-fast, his crew-cut head bobbing as he sidestepped the attack, but the cluttered space worked against him. A half-painted replica of a Victorian chaise lounge became his unintended stumbling block, sending him reeling backward with a curse.

"Elle!" he barked, regaining his footing just as Robert turned on her.

She had already positioned herself defensively, her mind processing the scene in fractions of seconds—the distance between them, the potential weapons among the debris, the likelihood of subduing Robert without causing serious harm.

The fight was a chaotic dance amidst the graveyard of artistic endeavors. Robert swung the prop sword, its edges menacing despite its theatrical origin. With each swing, Elle dodged, her dark hair streaked with white flashing under the dim warehouse lights. Her movements were practiced, precise; there was no room for error in this unpredictable chaos she so detested.

"Enough!" she commanded, feinting to the left then sweeping low to avoid another erratic slash. Her voice was sharp, piercing through the commotion, yet Robert's frenzied state seemed beyond the reach of reason.

His next move was a poorly judged thrust, overextended and desperate. Elle seized the opportunity. The combat skills ingrained in her muscle memory during FBI training surged to the forefront. She closed the gap between them, sidestepping the blade and redirecting Robert's momentum to unbalance him.

Her hand shot out, swift as a striking viper, finding the exposed wrist that held the makeshift weapon. A twist, a step, and a controlled application of force—a technique perfected in countless hours of practice—and the prop clattered onto the concrete floor. She kicked it away, far out of Robert's reach.

"Stop this madness," she said, breathing steady despite the adrenaline that coursed through her veins. "We're not here to harm you."

Robert, disarmed and panting, looked at her with a mixture of shock and uncomprehending fear. Elle's heart raced, but her stance remained unyielding.

Tom lunged forward, the muscles in his arms flexing as he grappled with Robert's flailing limbs. Elle could see the determination etched into her partner's scarred face, a silent testament to his lineage of law enforcement. His crew-cut hair seemed to bristle with focus, his body moving with a grace that belied his imposing form.

"Elle!" Tom barked, just as Robert's elbow swung towards him.

Springing into action, Elle circled behind the struggling men. She whipped out her handcuffs, the metallic click slicing through the tension. With precision, she snapped one cuff around Robert's wrist, feeling the tautness of his tendons under his clammy skin.

"Got him," she breathed, securing the second cuff as Tom finally pinned Robert to the ground. The fight left Robert's body in a sudden whoosh, his chest heaving against the cold floor.

"Stay down, Brown. It's over," Tom growled, maintaining pressure on the subdued man.

Elle stood back up, scanning the warehouse as Tom kept Robert under control. Her walnut hair, streaked prematurely white at the bangs, clung to her forehead, damp from exertion. Despite the adrenaline, her mind was clear, her eyes sharp, taking in every detail.

Piles of scripts lay scattered across a makeshift desk, their pages fluttering like specters in the draft. Costumes hung from racks, swaying gently—a macabre dance of fabric and shadow. Props were strewn haphazardly, a graveyard of discarded ideas and unfulfilled potential.

Robert continued to wriggle beneath Tom's hold, his voice rising in panicked crescendos. "I didn't do anything! You've got it all wrong!"

Elle ignored him. Items spoke more truth than people, especially crazed, prop sword-wielding people. Elle knelt beside a toppled stack of papers, her fingers brushing over the edges as she searched for any clue, any piece of evidence that could cement Robert's guilt. Her parents had instilled the importance of truth in her from a young age, and she clung to it now as a beacon in the murkiness of their investigation.

"Look for something out of place, something that doesn't fit," she murmured to herself, remembering her cryptography training—patterns were everywhere if you knew how to look.

"Elle?" Tom's voice pulled her back to the present.

"Keep him there," she said, not looking up as she continued her methodical search. Her fingertips grazed a script with an unusually heavy paperweight on top. She lifted it, revealing a series of notes scrawled in the margins.

"Could this be...?" she pondered aloud, her code-breaking instincts piqued as she scrutinized the annotations.

"Elle," Tom repeated, a note of urgency in his voice. He had noticed her sudden interest.

"Give me a second, Tom," she replied, absorbed in the cryptic writings. Very similar to the pages they'd found at the crime scenes.

But the same?

Hard to tell. The writing was cramped and hurried. The ink was the same color...

As she worked, the cacophony of Robert's pleas faded into the background. Elle's world narrowed to the patterns before her, the familiar comfort of codes and the undying quest for truth guiding her steady hand.

Elle's gaze swept across the warehouse, a landscape of chaos laid bare by their recent scuffle. Strewn amongst the debris of the fight, she discovered fragments of Robert's psyche—a myriad of half-constructed stage sets and grotesque props that spoke volumes of his fascination with the macabre. Tattered scripts lay abandoned beside skull replicas, while a guillotine prop loomed ominously in a darkened corner, its blade catching the faint light that seeped into the room.

She navigated through the wreckage, her boots crunching over splintered wood, feeling the weight of evidence pile up around her. The scenes depicted were too familiar, resonating with the sinister flair of the murders they were investigating. Her mind ticked away, processing every detail. Could these be mere coincidences or the morbid inspirations of a killer?

"Look at this," she called to Tom, pointing toward a collage of unsettling images pinned haphazardly to a board. Newspaper clippings of historical tragedies interwoven with lines from Shakespearean plays, each annotated with fervid scribbles that only someone deeply entrenched in drama would appreciate—or mimic.

"Quite the love affair with death," Tom muttered, following her line of sight.

"Or an obsession," Elle countered, her voice tinged with the clinical detachment she reserved for analyzing crime scenes.

Yet, as she turned back to Robert, who was now slumped against a wall, his struggle had subsided into shallow, ragged breaths. Their eyes met, and Elle caught a glimpse of something raw and unfiltered in his. It wasn't the smug satisfaction of a criminal mastermind; it was stark, paralyzing fear.

"Robert Brown, you're not what I expected," she said softly, her blunt honesty surfacing without filter.

She had her phone in hand, and compared the images of the annotated pages from the previous crime scenes to the handwriting in the margins of *these* plays.

No match.

She scowled, leaning in closer.

The handwriting was similar, but not an exact match. Elle's brow furrowed as she tried to make sense of the discrepancies. Something didn't add up. She had been so sure that Robert was their guy, the connection they had been searching for.

"Elle, we need to process him," Tom's voice broke through her concentration, his tone urgent.

She looked up at him, confusion evident in her eyes. "But Tom, this doesn't make sense. The handwriting, the themes—it all seemed so promising."

Tom's grip tightened on Robert's arm.

Elle hesitated for a moment, torn between her instinct to pursue the truth and the practicality of the situation. Reluctantly, she nodded and pocketed the annotated pages.

She turned finally to face their suspect.

He was staring at them, wide-eyed.

"Tell me about Laura Davis," Elle said softly.

"Who?" he retorted.

"Tell me about Rebecca. About Sarah."

"I don't know these women," he retorted.

Was he telling the truth? The handwriting didn't match. She hesitated. "I need a writing sample," she said simply.

"W-what?"

"Right now. You can clear some things up if you provide a sample." She shrugged.

He blinked, glancing down at his cuffed hands, then up again.

"You sure about this?" Tom muttered.

But she simply nodded once.

Elle watched as Robert hesitated, his gaze shifting between her and Tom. She could see the turmoil in his eyes, the fear mixed with a stubborn refusal to comply.

"I didn't do anything," he whispered, his voice barely audible.

Elle took a step closer, her eyes locked with his. "Prove it," she said firmly.

Reluctantly, Robert extended his trembling hand and reached for the pen Elle offered. As he began to write, Elle studied his movements, her analytical mind absorbing every detail. The strokes of the pen were hesitant and shaky, but there was a certain fluidity to them that caught her attention.

Once Robert finished writing, Elle carefully took the paper from him and examined it side by side with the annotated pages she had found at the other crime scenes.

No match. No. She had an eye for handwriting, and part of her cryptography training involved a study in handwriting. The letters were too cramped, and the P's had a swirl which didn't align with the previous pages. Elle's mind raced, trying to make sense of the undeniable differences in the handwriting. She had been so sure that they were on the right track with Robert, but now she found herself questioning everything.

"Elle," Tom spoke up, breaking the tense silence in the room. "Do you think we've got the wrong guy?"

She sighed, her shoulders slumping slightly. "I don't know, Tom. The evidence seemed to point in his direction, but this... it just doesn't match."

Tom glanced at Robert, who was watching them both with a mix of confusion and desperation. "What do we do now?"

Elle's mind whirled with possibilities. If Robert wasn't their killer, then who was? And why had they left behind those annotated pages at each crime scene? It was as if someone was intentionally leading them astray, planting false evidence to divert their attention.

Their suspect's eyes widened, a silent plea etched within them. "You don't understand," he gasped, his voice hoarse. "I create art—I don't imitate life with death."

Elle studied him, the gears in her mind grinding to a halt. Was this the face of a misunderstood artist or a clever facade?

She voiced her hesitation. "There's more to this than theatrics."

"Or we've got our man, and he's playing us," Tom replied.

"Maybe," Elle conceded, but her instincts whispered otherwise. She examined Robert's bindings, ensuring they weren't too tight, her actions guided by protocol but softened by uncertainty.

"Keep your head clear, Elle," she reminded herself silently. "Codes are truth. And the truth is rarely wrapped in a neat bow."

Elle's steps echoed through the cavernous space of the warehouse as she and Tom escorted Robert toward the exit. The clink of the handcuffs was a stark counterpoint to the silence that had fallen, a sharp reminder of the chaos that had just unfolded.

She glanced back over her shoulder at the shadowy interior. Half-constructed stage sets loomed like specters, props strewn haphazardly across the floor—the aftermath of their scuffle. The disarray seemed to mock her, whispering of clues overlooked and secrets still ensconced in the dim corners.

"Keep moving," Tom said to Robert, his voice low but firm as he nudged the cuffed man forward.

Elle felt the weight of Robert's gaze, heavy with a plea for understanding. She turned away; focusing on the task at hand was imperative, yet her mind refused to quiet. There was something unsatisfying about this victory, an itch in her brain where the pieces didn't quite fit.

They passed under a steel beam, its surface rusted from years of neglect—an apt metaphor for the once-celebrated director now shackled and subdued. The cold bite of the metal handcuffs against Robert's wrists seemed too real, too harsh against the backdrop of his fabricated worlds.

"Almost there," Tom muttered, though to whom it wasn't clear.

The outside light began to spill into the warehouse entrance, casting elongated shadows that danced along the walls. Elle's eyes swept over the scene one last time, hunting for the anomaly in this chaotic tapestry. It was here, she could feel it—hidden in plain sight, much like the solitary white streak in her dark hair that defied conformity.

"Why did you attack us?" Ellse said suddenly.

"Hmm? Did I?" he looked confused.

Or crazed.

Was he simply an insane artist off his medication? Were they making a mistake?

Her training told her to move on, to follow protocol and leave no stone unturned later. Yet, intuition tugged at her, a silent alarm that buzzed beneath her skin.

"Elle?" Tom's questioning tone brought her attention back to the present.

"Nothing," she replied, a bit too quickly. "Just making sure we're not missing anything."

As they stepped out into the daylight, the chill from the warehouse's shadows gave way to the warmth of the sun. But warmth did nothing to thaw the cold knot of doubt lodged in Elle's stomach. Even as Robert's silhouette shrank against the light, the enigma he represented grew larger, casting a long shadow over their supposed triumph.

"Let's get him to the bureau," Tom said, breaking the momentary silence.

Elle nodded, her gaze lingering on the threshold of the warehouse. The truth was out there, possibly etched into the very walls they were leaving behind. And Elle Keen hated loose ends. The code of this case remained undeciphered, and every fiber of her being yearned to crack it wide open.

"I didn't hurt anyone," the director was saying. "I... I swear it! I swear it!" he was screaming now, frothing at the mouth, bucking his hips, and trying desperately to escape.

Tom tried to wrangle him, and Elle stood aside, watching.

Her mind often reacted before her physical body. Tom was the opposite, he was already coralling their suspect towards the car while Elle watched. But stagnancy of body didn't mean stagnancy of mind.

Did this man really match the profile they'd come up with? The killer was a narcist. he cared deeply about apperances, and how he was perceived.

But Robert...

Robert, with his disheveled hair and wild eyes, seemed anything but concerned with appearances. Elle's brows furrowed as she pondered the contradiction. Could it be a ruse? A clever act to throw them off his trail? Or was he truly innocent?

She bit her lower lip, a habit that always surfaced when uncertainty clouded her thoughts. Her gaze lingered on the fleeting glimmers of desperation in Robert's eyes. There was something there—a flicker of vulnerability that didn't quite fit the profile they had constructed.

As the car door slammed shut and the engine roared to life, Elle made a split-second decision. "Tom, wait!" she called out, her voice tinged with urgency.

Tom glanced at her through the rearview mirror, his eyes reflecting surprise. "What is it, Elle?"

"I don't think we have the whole picture," she said, her words laced with conviction. "There's something off about this case, about Robert."

Tom's grip tightened on the steering wheel as he took in Elle's words. "You think we got it wrong?"

Elle nodded slowly. "I can't shake this feeling that there's more at play here—something we've overlooked."

Her partner's brows knitted together in concern, but he didn't question her instincts. That was one of the things she appreciated most about Tom—he trusted her judgment.

"Where are we going then?" he asked, redirecting the vehicle away from the Bureau.

Elle's mind raced, searching for a clue or any inkling that might lead them closer to unraveling the truth.

Elle's eyes narrowed as she watched Robert's desperate struggle in the rearview mirror, where he bucked and swayed in the backseat, weeping now. A pang of pity resounded in her chest, which was blunted somewhat by the memory of him lunging at her with a sword, attempting to impale her heart.

"I didn't hurt anyone!" he moaned. There was a rawness to his words, a desperation that tugged at her heartstrings. Could he truly be innocent? The doubts gnawed at her, threatening to unravel the careful threads of their investigation.

"We need to know the truth," Elle murmured under her breath, more to herself than anyone else.

Tom glanced at her, concern etched into the lines of his face. "What are you thinking, Elle?"

She stared at Robert, studying the intensity in his eyes. "I think we might have missed something. Something crucial."

Her partner's brows furrowed as he considered her words. "You want to go back in?"

Elle shook her head, her mind already racing with possibilities. If there was a chance that Robert was innocent, she couldn't afford to ignore it.

"Call for backup," she said, her voice firm and unwavering. "Let them take pictures of everything. "We need to talk to Robert. See what's under the surface."

He seemed to hear her and briefly paused his caterwauling to meet her gaze in the rearview mirror.

He frowned at her. And she frowned back.

Was this all an act?

Quite possibly. And it was up to her to find out.

"Next stop, interrogation room," she muttered. "And tell backup to photograph *everything*. I mean everything."

Tom nodded, already radioing in their next step.

CHAPTER FIFTEEN

The buzz of fluorescent lights overhead mingled with the distant murmur of activity outside the cramped, windowless room—a stark contrast to the gravity within its walls. Elle Keen flicked through the dossier one more time, her fingers tracing the sharp black-and-white photos and meticulous notes that had coalesced into the labyrinthine profile of Robert Brown.

Tom Wright leaned back against the steel table, arms folded across his broad chest, the tailored blue suit stretching over his muscles. "Maybe we don't play games," he said, his voice steady and sure. "We be direct, cut straight through the crap. He's used to people dancing around him, trying to act and perform."

Elle nodded, closing the file with a snap. Her eyes met Tom's, finding an echo of her own determination in his dark, focused stare. "Directness. He might respect that," she conceded. "But we can't come off aggressive. That's what he wants—a fight."

"Agreed." Tom pushed off from the table, his movements fluid despite his muscular build. "So we start slow, talk about the things he loves. The literature, the artistry of words—Shakespeare was it?"

"Exactly," Elle replied, standing up and smoothing the front of her blazer. "Lure him into a sense of intellectual camaraderie, then pivot to Laura Davis. We need him to slip, show us something real."

"Remember," Tom added, pausing by the door, his hand on the knob, "he enjoys the dance, even when he pretends not to. Let's give him one he can't resist."

"Lead with empathy, follow with evidence," Elle affirmed, a slight curve touching the corner of her lips. It was a dance indeed, and they were about to step onto the floor.

The hum of hushed conversations washed over Elle as she stepped into the observation room, a space alive with the nervous energy of anticipation. Her gaze cut through the semi-darkness to the silhouette of Robert Brown, seated in the adjacent interrogation chamber. He was an island of calm in a sea of scrutiny, his posture relaxed, almost arrogantly so, as he waited behind the one-way mirror.

All signs of his reactions in the car had faded. Maybe she'd been wrong about his profile after all. Maybe he desperately did are about how he was perceived.

Tom nudged her arm, and Elle refocused, scanning the array of law enforcement officers who clustered around the monitoring equipment. Their eyes were glued to Robert, each movement he made, every slight shift in expression, captured and analyzed. Whispers of conjecture and the soft clicks of keyboards formed a backdrop to the visual ballet playing out before them.

"Showtime," murmured Tom, a subtle cue that it was time to peel away the layers of this enigma named Robert Brown.

Elle felt the familiar thrum of adrenaline as she pushed open the door to the interrogation room. The air was thick with the weight of unspoken questions, the walls lingering in aura with the ghosts of confessions past. She ignored the chair meant for her and leaned casually against the table, leveling her gaze at Robert.

"Good evening, Mr. Brown," Elle began, her voice measured, betraying none of the tension coiled within her. "I'm Agent Keen, and I want to thank you for your cooperation tonight."

Robert's eyes held hers, a flicker of curiosity—or was it amusement?—dancing within their depths. "Agent Keen," he echoed, tasting her name like it was a riddle to be solved. "How can I be of assistance?"

He was practically a different man than he'd been back in his theater. A reserved, quite, astute man. He stared at her quizically. A small, confient smile played on his lips. Gone was the madness in his eyes, the frothing, the wailing.

Strange. He was an actor. she had to remember that.

"Let's start with something easy," she said, easing into the rhythm of dialogue. "Your work. You're a director, correct?"

"That's right," Robert replied, tilting his head slightly. His fingers drummed a silent sonnet on the tabletop. "Shakespearean tragedies, primarily."

"Must be fascinating," Elle commented, her tone genuine. She remembered her mother's linguistic puzzles, the way words could conceal and reveal simultaneously. "To immerse yourself in such complex human emotions every day."

"Indeed," Robert mused, a smile ghosting his lips. "One could say it offers a unique perspective on the human condition."

"Perspective," Elle repeated, allowing the word to hang between them as a bridge to deeper discourse. "That's what we're all after, isn't it?" She folded her hands in front of her, projecting calm authority. "Understanding why people do the things they do."

"An eternal quest, Agent Keen," Robert agreed. There was a spark in his eye, a sign that perhaps she had begun to weave the threads of rapport.

"Tell me about your personal life, Mr. Brown," Elle ventured, maintaining the illusion of casual interest. "Any hobbies outside of the world of plays?"

Robert leaned back, considering her question. "Well, life often imitates art, doesn't it? Or is it the other way around?"

"Perhaps we'll find out," Elle said, the corner of her mouth lifting just enough to suggest camaraderie but not enough to invite familiarity. She sensed the ebb and flow of the intellectual dance Tom had hinted at, a prelude to the crescendo of truth they sought.

Elle leaned forward, her dark eyes locked onto Robert's with the intensity of a seasoned agent. The initial pleasantries had quickly descended into a chess match, with each of Robert's answers circling around the truth like a vulture above carrion, never quite landing.

"Mr. Brown," she began, her voice harboring a sharper edge now, "let's discuss your relationship with Laura Davis." Elle watched as his brows knitted together, a subtle but defiant barrier against her inquiry.

"Relationship?" he scoffed, tilting his head ever so slightly. "You flatter me, Agent Keen. I don't know anyone by that name."

"And yet, I can't help but notice on your blog post, you'd been to see a play she was in."

"Oh? Which one?'

"Othello. And here, a few months before, A Midsummer Night's Dream." Elle turned a printout of the blog post in question towards their suspect. "I can't help but notice you weren't particularly nice in your comments. You got into an argument, it says here, with one of the actors. Was it Laura?"

Robert's lips twitched, a micro-expression betraying irritation. "Theater arguments are hardly uncommon, Agent. Especially when discussing Shakespeare."

"Ah, yes," Elle leaned back, folding her arms as she conjured the image of a dagger from 'Macbeth.' "Shakespearean drama—full of betrayal, revenge, murder. Does your interest in such themes extend beyond academic appreciation?"

He held her gaze, the ghost of a smirk playing on his face. "One can appreciate the darkness of the human soul without indulging in it."

"Indulge me then," Elle said, her voice cold as steel. "Your fascination with the Bard's more... lethal narratives. Does it not strike you as peculiar, given our current discourse?"

"Life is but a walking shadow," Robert quoted, his eyes glinting with the recital. "A poor player that struts and frets his hour upon the stage."

"Then let's not strut, Mr. Brown," Elle interjected, determined to cut through his performance. "Let's speak plainly about your connection to Laura. A shared interest in literature doesn't explain why your fingerprints were found on a book in her apartment—a rare edition of 'Othello,' I believe."

Robert's demeanor remained unflappable, yet there was a tightening around his eyes, a sign that she may have finally struck a chord. Elle knew she was close, inching toward the vulnerability in Robert's armor. He was intelligent, undoubtedly, but so was she—and she would not be dissuaded by eloquence or evasion.

"An honest tale speeds best being plainly told," she concluded, invoking the words of the Bard himself, watching as Robert's façade wavered ever so faintly under the weight of her scrutiny.

Elle leaned forward, elbows on the cold metal table, her dark eyes locked onto Robert's. The tightness around his eyes had dissipated, replaced once more by an unsettling calm. She flicked a glance at Tom where he stood by the door and who gave a subtle nod, before returning her focus to the man across from her.

"Let's talk about the night of March 22nd," Elle said, voice steady. "Your neighbors reported seeing you return home late. Unusual for a Tuesday evening, wasn't it?"

Robert folded his hands on the table, the ghost of a smile touching his lips. "My habits are my own, Agent Keen. A man is entitled to his nocturnal idiosyncrasies, wouldn't you agree?"

"Unless those 'idiosyncrasies' involve murder," Elle shot back.

"Accusations require proof, Agent. And I believe you're short on that commodity."

Elle's jaw clenched momentarily, but she maintained her composure. There was a rhythm to this dance, and she refused to be led. "We have more than you think, Robert. Enough to keep peeling back the layers until we find what's rotting underneath."

"Layers, you say?" Robert mused, tilting his head slightly. "And yet, here we are, talking in circles."

"Only because you're avoiding the path leading straight to the truth," Elle retorted. Her mind raced—each question was a code to crack, each answer a potential cipher. Her parents would have approached it like a complex equation, layers upon layers to unravel. She felt that same drive now, the pursuit of a solution just beyond reach.

"Truth," he echoed, as if tasting the word. "A relative term, don't you think?"

"Not when it comes to life and death."

"Ah, but death is merely the ultimate truth, isn't it?"

Elle leaned back, her expression unreadable. She let the silence stretch between them, watching as Robert settled back into his chair, defiant in his cryptic responses. It was a game of chess, and he was guarding his king with a row of pawns lined up neatly in front.

"Perhaps," she finally said, "but Laura Davis's death won't be your checkmate."

"Nor will it be your crowning achievement," Robert replied smoothly. "As for prints on a book? I read many books. I go to many libraries. I'm sure she may have checked out a book I once borrowed. Simple enough."

Frustration simmered under the surface, but Elle knew better than to let it bubble over.

"Oh? Is that the excuse?"

"No excuse."

"How long ago did you borrow Othello?"

"I don't remember?"

"Can you give me a timeframe?"

"Time," Robert mused, "is the least reliable witness."

Elle's hands rested flat on the metallic surface of the table. The cold air of the interrogation room seemed to accentuate the severity of her tone. She locked eyes with Robert, and for a moment, there was a crackling silence as she prepared her next calculated assault.

"Let's talk about Laura Davis," Elle said, her voice slicing through the stillness. "She had aspirations, a future – until someone decided she didn't deserve either."

Robert's gaze didn't waver, his lips pressing into a thin line.

"Interesting that they found a copy of Hamlet by her body," Elle continued, pressing on the tender nerve of literature. "A book you've been known to quote extensively. Coincidence, don't you think?" Elle pushed further, her words sharpening like knives. "Especially since we both know your fascination with Shakespeare's darkest themes."

"Life’s but a walking shadow," Robert quipped, the corners of his mouth twitching upwards ever so slightly.

"Except shadows don't leave traces, Mr. Brown. And right now, all traces point to you," Elle retorted.

She leaned in, invading his space with the weight of her presence, and continued, "Your prints were found on that book. You still haven't explained it."

His composure was a mask, unyielding and immaculate as ever. "I've told you, Agent Keen, I frequent many bookstores and libraries. It's hardly damning evidence."

Elle scrutinized him, searching for any sign of faltering. But he sat before her, the picture of stoic indifference. As she pressed on with the details of Laura's demise, a part of her studied Robert's response, or lack thereof, with the precision of a cryptographer decoding an enigma.

"Laura was heard arguing with a man about Shakespeare, the night she died," Elle said, throwing down her ace. "Witnesses say the man quoted 'Hamlet' before storming off."

"Words, words, words," Robert muttered, echoing Hamlet's own disillusionment.

"Exactly," Elle replied sharply. "And those words are all we have left of Laura Davis."

Despite the incriminating facts, Robert's demeanor remained as solid as bedrock. It frustrated Elle, but she couldn't help but admire the way he clung to his narrative with a vice-like grip.

"Am I to be judged by my literary tastes?" Robert asked calmly. "Are we not allowed our passions without being condemned?"

"Passion is one thing," Elle said, straightening up. "Obsession that leads to murder is another."

"Then you must be obsessed with me," he shot back quickly, "considering the fervor with which you pursue this baseless accusation."

"Do you have an alibi?"

"I live alone. I act alone. No. You know I don't."

He glared at her, a defiance in his gaze.

She shifted uncomfortably, trying to read the man sitting before her.

Her hands tightened and untightened. She shifted side to side, discomfort in every twitch and fidget.

Could he be telling the truth?

A print on a book he'd borrowed? Accidentally showing up at Laura's apartment?

The Shakespearean connections?

It all seemed like too much. It seemed silly.

"I had a play, though," he said suddenly.

"Excuse me?"

"Two nights in the last week. A play."

"Which day did this murder occur on?"

"Why didn't you mention a play before?"

He shrugged dismissively. "I forgot."

"Sure you did," she muttered.

"So which day?" he pressed.

"That's not how this works. You tell *me* which day you were occupied."

He shrugged. "A room full of witnesses, mind. A private monologue. I performed the role of Macbeth."

Elle's eyes narrowed, her mind racing to piece everything together. A play. A room full of witnesses. His obsession with Shakespeare's darkest themes. Could it be that Robert had an alibi for Laura Davis's murder? But even as this possibility danced at the edges of her thoughts, a nagging doubt lingered.

"And where was this play performed?" she asked, her voice laced with skepticism.

"At a small theater downtown," he replied coolly. "A group of aspiring actors performing for a handful of theater enthusiasts."

Elle's heart sank. If Robert could substantiate his alibi, then all the evidence they had gathered against him would crumble like a house of cards. She knew she couldn't dismiss this lead, but doubts still gnawed at her.

"I was busy Monday and Saturday night," he said simply.

She froze. Saturday was the night Laura had died. Did he know? Was it just more performance?

"I can prove it," he added simply. "I was recorded on my phone by a friend. I wanted to see my own performance... It helps me to grow as an actor."

Elle clicked her fingers, and Tom hastened over with the suspect's phone. She pushed it towards Robert so he could unlock it.

He did so slowly, dramatically, as if even this were another performance. His lips had twisted into a smirk.

Elle's heart raced as she watched Robert input his passcode with deliberate slowness. The screen of his phone illuminated, revealing a collection of apps and notifications. She held her breath, waiting for him to open the video that would either confirm or dismantle his alibi.

With an air of self-assuredness, Robert swiped through his videos until he landed on one labeled "Macbeth Performance." He tapped it with precision, and the video began to play. Elle fixated on the screen, her eyes scanning the footage for any sign of deception.

As the scene unfolded before her, she found herself slipping into the world of Shakespearean tragedy. Robert's voice reverberated through the speakers of his phone, reciting Macbeth's infamous soliloquy as he paced across the stage. The passion in his delivery was undeniable.

Elle exchanged a glance with Tom, who stood beside her, equally transfixed by what they were witnessing. She stared most at the timestamp. Smack dab in the middle of the frame the coroner had provided for Laura's death.

He'd been in a theater across town. The video seemed to be an ironclad alibi for Robert. It showed him in plain sight, performing on stage among a group of actors who were captivated by his portrayal.

The doubt that had plagued Elle's mind began to dissipate, replaced by a newfound clarity. Maybe Robert wasn't the killer after all. Maybe their focus on him had blinded them to other possibilities and allowed the true culprit to remain hidden.

She glanced back at Robert, expecting to find arrogance or triumph in his eyes. Instead, what she saw was a glimmer of vulnerability—uncertainty that betrayed his stoic demeanor.

"You can verify with the theater," he said quietly, practically pleading for them to believe him.

Elle bit her lip, feeling a jolt of pain.

Without another word, she marched out of the room.

CHAPTER SIXTEEN

Elle shifted uncomfortably, and glanced over towards where her partner wathced her from the front seat.

"I'm fine handling it," Tom said quietly. "You can stay back. It's fine."

She scowled. "Don't need the kid gloves, Tom. I'm fine."

He eyed her as they drove towards Linda O'Malley's home. Sarah Mason's roommate was the closest person in the city to kin that their latest victim had. And now, the two of them were hastening to her residence, leaving behind the tangle of confusion they'd uncovered in the interrogation room.

Cops were still interviewing their actor turned self-proclaimed director. And Elle couldn't ignore the obvious connections. The fingerprint on a book. The sword he'd attacked agents with... his obsession with the theater...

But his alibi was ironclad.

Still... maybe he'd hired someone. Maybe he had an accomplice?

If so, they needed to find out. They needed more information.

"Ready?" Tom asked, meeting her gaze.

"Lisa won't see it coming," Elle said, her fingers tracing the edge of her badge that sat heavily against her chest.

"Nobody does," Tom murmured, pushing open the door to the parking lot, where the sun cast long shadows on the concrete. "We'll get through it together."

The drive to the apartment complex was filled with an uneasy silence, both agents lost in their thoughts.

As they parked, Elle felt the familiar grip of her gun against her hip, a grim comfort. They approached the building with a sense of purpose, despite the dread that gnawed at Elle's resolve. She couldn't help but wonder if they were walking into just another chapter of sorrow or if Lisa's words would unravel the cipher of the killer's motive.

"Elle," Tom said softly, bringing her back to the present. "Let's do what we came here for."

With a nod, Elle stepped forward, preparing to trade the solace of unanswered questions for the harsh reality of speaking the unspeakable.

They were about to shatter a world, and from those shards, they hoped to piece together enough to catch a killer. It was a brutal balance, one they tread with every name they had to cross off their list. But today, as they climbed the steps to Lisa's door, the burden seemed heavier, the path ahead more obscure than ever.

The rhythm of children's laughter punctuated the air as Elle and Tom made their way up the bustling courtyard of the apartment complex. Balconies overflowed with potted plants, and the scent of someone's dinner wafted down from an open window, a stark contrast to the sterile tang of crime scenes they had become accustomed to. Elle felt the discordant hum of life around her, a cacophony that made the silence they were about to impart all the more profound.

They climbed the stairs, each step resonating with the echo of vibrant living—a dog barking, a couple arguing passionately in Spanish, a baby crying—all these threads of existence weaving an intricate tapestry so at odds with the finality of death. Elle's mind reeled, juxtaposing this everyday symphony with the funereal stillness that awaited them inside Lisa's apartment.

At the door, Tom paused, his hand hovering over the buzzer. Elle caught his eye, a silent exchange passing between them—this was the hardest part of the job, and it never got any easier. He pressed the button, the buzz a jarring note amidst the melody of life in the complex.

A voice crackled over the speaker. "Who is it?"

"FBI," Tom replied, his tone steady but empathetic. "We need to speak with Lisa regarding Sarah Mason."

There was a moment of silence, the anticipation heavy in the air. Then, with a click, the door unlocked, and they stepped into the dimly lit hallway.

A door at the far end creaked and rattled as a chain or bolt was undone.

The door swung open, revealing Lisa, her eyes wide with an instinctual alarm as she took in the sight of two FBI agents on her threshold. The glow from the television flickered across her face, casting shadows that seemed to accentuate her sudden fear. On screen, a laugh track rolled incongruously from a sitcom, its cheerfulness a grotesque backdrop to the gravity of their presence.

"Lisa?" Elle's voice was modulated, carefully neutral, yet beneath the surface lay a coil of empathetic tension. She knew the power of what they were about to unleash, the irreversible alteration of Lisa's world.

"Y-yes?" Lisa's voice trembled, her fingers clutching the doorframe. "Is everything okay?"

Tom offered a sympathetic half-smile, one that failed to reach his eyes. "May we come in for a moment? It's important."

As they stepped into the small, lived-in space, the contrast between life and death, light and dark, comedy and tragedy played out before them, the scene set for the truth to unfold.

Elle settled onto the edge of a threadbare couch, her posture open, non-threatening. Tom leaned against a wall nearby, his presence solid and reassuring. The room felt charged with an expectancy that made Elle's heart thrum in her chest.

"Lisa," Elle began, her voice a soft whisper, "there's no easy way to say this." She paused, giving space for the words to settle. "Sarah... Sarah was found dead last night."

The color drained from Lisa's face as if the words were a physical blow. Her lips parted, but no sound emerged. For a moment, she seemed frozen, her eyes darting between Elle and Tom, seeking a contradiction that would not come.

"Dead?" Lisa's voice finally broke the silence, a fragile echo of denial. "No, that can't be. I just saw her—she must have... It has to be a mistake!"

Tears pooled and fell freely down her cheeks, her body beginning to tremble. Elle reached out, her hand hovering, unsure if the contact would be welcomed. Lisa collapsed inward, wrapping her arms around herself, sinking into the depth of her grief.

Tom, unlike Elle, didn't hesitate to comfort. He stepped forward, gently placing a calloused hand on the woman's shoulder. "It's sorry," he said quietly. "I'm so, so, very sorry. Lisa, I'm so sorry," Tom said, his own voice thick with empathy, the years of delivering such news never hardening him to its impact.

Elle watched uncomfortably, wishing she knew how to comfort the way her partner did. She reached out, stiffly, tapping Lisa on the arm, but quickly withdrawing her hand as if she'd scalded herself.

Silence enveloped the room, punctuated only by the muffled sounds of laughter still emanating from the forgotten television show. Elle noted the remote on the couch, hastened over and muted the screen, restoring some semblance of solemnity to the room.

"Can you tell us about the last time you saw Sarah?" Elle asked gently after a respectful pause, as Tom guided Lisa back to the couch. They sat together, Tom's demeanor patient and kind. "Anything you remember could help us understand what happened."

Lisa wiped her tears, sniffling as she tried to compose herself. "She was... she was excited about an audition," she managed through sobs. "Always chasing her dreams, you know? She left smiling... How is this possible?"

"Did she meet anyone new recently, someone who might have wanted to harm her?" Elle probed softly, her mind cataloging every inflection, every detail that might hint at a pattern or motive.

"No, no one," Lisa replied, her brow furrowing as she searched through her memories. "She was cautious, always careful about who she let into her life."

"Think carefully, Lisa. Even something that seems trivial could be important," Tom interjected, his tone gentle yet firm.

Lisa shook her head, frustration and sorrow mingling in her expression. "I just... I can't think of anything. Everything was normal, just... normal."

"Normal" was a word Elle had learned to distrust in her line of work, but she nodded understandingly, offering a small, sad smile. In the silence, they each bore the weight of the unsaid, the reality that "normal" was often a veneer for something far more sinister.

Elle observed the subtle shift in Lisa's posture, a straightening of her back and a distant focus in her eyes, as if she was about to share something sacred. "Sarah acted in plays," Lisa said, and the words seemed to pull her from the depths of her sorrow for a moment. "She was so alive on stage... just last month, she played Juliet in Shakespeare's 'Romeo and Juliet'."

"Did she enjoy it?" Elle asked, her voice low but eager, as if trying not to startle a revelation out of hiding.

"More than anything," Lisa replied, a faint smile breaking through her tears. It was a smile that spoke of pride in her late friend's passions. "She said it made her feel like she could escape into someone else's life for a while."

Tom exhaled softly, his brow furrowing in thought. "Was there anyone unusual involved in the theatre scene, maybe someone who took a particular interest in Sarah?"

"No, it was a small community theatre. Everyone knew everyone," Lisa answered, but Elle noted the brief hesitation before she spoke, storing it away like a puzzle piece to be examined later.

"Would you mind if we take a look at her room?" Elle asked, her tone shifting into her professional cadence. "There might be something there that can help us understand what happened."

Lisa nodded mutely, rising from the couch with a grace that belied her turmoil. She led Elle and Tom to Sarah's room, opening the door to reveal an intimate portrait of the young woman they were coming to know posthumously.

The room was neat, almost meticulously so, with books aligned at right angles on the shelves and a bulletin board laden with photos of smiling faces and theatre playbills. The bed was made tightly, the comforter pulled taut enough to bounce a quarter off, and atop it lay a well-thumbed copy of "Romeo and Juliet" with a silk rose bookmark peering out from its pages.

As Elle scanned the room, her keen eyes picked up on the subtleties—the array of makeup brushes meticulously cleaned and organized, the wardrobe filled with contemporary and vintage clothing, a mix of practicality and whimsy. It was eerily reminiscent of the other victims: creative souls with lives steeped in artistry and careful order—a pattern emerging from chaos.

"Notice anything?" Tom murmured, his presence near but unobtrusive.

"The precision," Elle responded, almost to herself. "It's like she was curating her own life, her own story. There's a desire here... to be seen, understood."

"Same as the others," Tom affirmed, his voice grim.

Elle's fingers hesitated above the playbill from Sarah's final performance as Juliet. Her mind raced, ciphering through this new information, decrypting the human code written in belongings left behind. In the margins of the script, annotations spoke of a young woman diving deeply into her character, perhaps revealing more about herself than she realized.

"Elle," Tom called quietly, nodding toward a wall adorned with candid shots of Sarah, each capturing a different facet of her essence.

Elle stepped closer, noting the similarity in Sarah's vibrant expression to those of previous victims captured in photographs at their respective crime scenes. It was a semblance too striking to ignore, a common thread woven intricately into the fabric of their fates.

"Whatever we're dealing with," Elle mused aloud, "it wants these women to be remembered, not just as victims, but as... muses."

"Someone obsessed with preserving their spirits," Tom added, his gaze lingering on the images.

"Or collecting them," Elle concluded, a hint of ice lacing her words.

Their shared glance held an understanding that transcended words. They were hunting a curator of tragedies, a collector of life's final acts, and now, armed with the knowledge of Sarah's passion for acting and her portrayal of Juliet, they had a new lead—a new angle in the profile of a killer.

A play... what if he'd seen her at the play? What if that was how he chose his victims?

"Every victim is distinct, yet... interchangeable in his eyes," Elle mused, her voice a soft whisper against the silence of the room. She let her gaze drift once more over the landscape of Sarah's existence—the books, the clothes, the lingering scent of ambition and youth cut tragically short.

"Let's pack it up," she said, finally tearing herself away from the scene that offered no answers. The weight of the unsolved case pressed heavily on her shoulders, an unwelcome burden that seemed to grow with each passing moment.

As they prepared to leave, Elle's phone shattered the quiet, its ringtone slicing through the despair that had settled around them. She glanced at the screen—SAIC Harper. Her pulse quickened; calls from the Special Agent in Charge were seldom harbingers of good news. She answered with a brisk, "Agent Keen."

"Elle, you need to get back here now," came the urgent reply, supervisor Harper's voice taut with restrained alarm. "The killer has made contact again. There's a message. It's coded, aimed specifically at us."

Tom watched as Elle's face tightened, the muscles around her jaw clenching visibly. This was her realm, the place where her unique aptitudes shone brightest. Codes were her sanctuary, a bastion of order amidst chaos. And yet, the notion that the killer was taunting them with these cryptic challenges stirred a storm of frustration within her—one that threatened to erode the very detachment that made her such an effective agent.

"Understood," she replied, her tone steady despite the turmoil brewing inside her. "We're on our way."

She ended the call, meeting Tom's questioning look with a nod that needed no words to convey its urgency. The game was changing, evolving with every move the killer made. But so too must they adapt, must they sharpen their focus until the truth could no longer hide behind riddles and shadows.

"Let's go," Elle said, a renewed determination steadying her voice. "A message was sent to the office."

"Message? What type of message," Tom asked, keeping his voice low so that Linda couldn't hear them from the adjoining room.

"Coded. But connected."

"Is it like the other ones?"

"It's like we said," she replied in a murmur. "he wants to be found. He wants the fame..."

"Well... let's oblige him then."

The two of them turned, preparing to bid farewell to Linda and hasten back to the FBI headquarters.

CHAPTER SEVENTEEN

The chill of the air-conditioned room did little to cool Elle's fevered mind as she and Tom shouldered their way through the clump of dark-suited agents. Eyes, as sharp as her intellect, fixed on the large screen that dominated the front wall of the task force headquarters. On it glowed the image of the latest taunt from a killer who was proving to be as much a master of puzzles as of death.

"Got something new?" Tom murmured, his voice low and steady—a stark contrast to the crackling energy that vibrated through the room.

Elle nodded curtly, not trusting herself to speak as she absorbed the digital representation of the crime scene. The photograph displayed a tableau that would have looked chaotic to the untrained eye, but to Elle, it was a scene etched with intention. A coded tapestry woven into a cruel and creative mockery of a final farewell. Symbols, numbers, and what appeared to be random marks created a sinister mosaic across the screen.

She studied it intently.

"See anything?" Tom murmured at her side.

Now that she'd arrived, more than one agent was glancing in her direction, studying her expression, searching for answers. This was her job, and everyone knew it. The cryptographer in their midst.

She stared at the images on the screen, frowning. Her memory sifted through the previous images she'd spotted at the crime scenes. Some of the symbols matched the annotations from the pages discovered at the crime scenes. There were snippets of sentences also displayed.

Each of them seemingly taken from Shakespearean work. She read:

"By the pricking of my thumbs, something wicked this way comes," Elle whispered, her eyes narrowing in concentration.

Tom leaned closer, his breath grazing her ear. "Macbeth," he murmured. "The Three Witches."

Elle nodded, her mind racing as she connected the dots.

She read the next line:

"Double, double toil and trouble; Fire burn and cauldron bubble."

Elle's heart skipped a beat. It was another line from Macbeth. The killer was deliberately using quotes from Shakespeare's play to taunt them. But why? What was the significance?

"I think we're dealing with someone who has a deep knowledge of literature," Elle said, her voice barely above a whisper.

Tom furrowed his brow. "We already knew that."

"No, we knew they had an interest. A fascination."

"So what are you saying?"

"I think they're smart. And educated."

"So an educated narcissist..."

"Yeah, that sounds right."

"I mean, these quotes aren't random," Elle explained.

"You think his next crime might be staged like Macbeth?"

"Maybe... I don't know. Or maybe he sees himself in Macbeth somehow."

"Which character?"

"Well, as we've said, he's a narccisist. So he could see himself as Macbeth, the tragic hero turned villain." Elle paused, her eyes still fixed on the screen. "But there's more to it than that. Macbeth is driven by ambition, consumed by his desire for power and greatness. Maybe this killer sees himself as the ultimate puppet master, pulling the strings to orchestrate these murders."

Tom's eyes widened with realization. "So these crimes are his way of proving his superior intellect and cunning?" he asked.

Elle nodded, a fierce determination burning in her eyes. "Exactly. He wants to show the world that he's playing a game, one that only he can win."

"We need to analyze the context of these quotes," Elle continued. "We need to understand what they signify in relation to the crimes and the victims."

She raised her phone, taking a screenshot of the image, then she turned, moving hastily to a quiet part of the station. As she did, she pulled out her phone, cycling to her e-reader and, after a quick, single tap purchase, she was perusing Macbeth.

The context of the two quotes... What were they?

Her memory was best suited to numbers, not letters. But as she sat in the breakroom, Tom joined her.

The two of them stared at the image he pulled up on the television screen. The brief quotes from Shakespeare surrounded by the intricate symbols and numbers.

She frowned.

"So," Tom said. "What's the context of the double-double, cauldron whatever line..."

Elle's mind raced as she flipped through the pages of Macbeth, searching for the context of the quotes. She finally found it—a conversation between the three witches in Act IV, Scene I. She quickly skimmed the dialogue, and her eyes widened with realization.

"It's about prophecies," Elle exclaimed, her voice tinged with excitement. "The witches are predicting Macbeth's future and giving him a false sense of security."

Tom leaned closer, his eyes fixed on the screen of Elle's e-reader. "What do you mean?"

Elle took a deep breath, reciting the lines from memory. "By the pricking of my thumbs, something wicked this way comes," she said. "The witches are hinting at Macbeth's downfall approaching."

Tom nodded, his expression growing more serious. "So the killer is using these quotes to foreshadow his next move?"

"Exactly," Elle replied, her voice filled with determination. "He wants to taunt us, to let us know that another murder is imminent."

Tom sighed and rubbed his temples. "But how do we use this information to stop him?"

Elle nodded. "Shakespeare's plays are known for their rich symbolism and intricate character relationships," she explained. "If we can decipher the hidden meanings behind these quotes, we might be able to find his next victim."

"Alright, so what about this next quote, here?"

Tom was pointing to another portion of the screen.

She peered at it and read:

"A dark and a hellish pit awaits the doomed souls."

Elle's brow furrowed as she repeated the words, trying to recall the source. She racked her brain, searching for the play that contained this quote. Suddenly, it clicked.

"That's from 'Hamlet'," she said with a mix of excitement and trepidation. "It's spoken by the ghost of King Hamlet, warning his son about the afterlife."

Tom leaned in closer, his eyes scanning the symbols and numbers that surrounded the quote. "So what does it mean? Is he telling us where he's going to strike next?"

Elle's mind whirled with possibilities. She knew that deciphering this quote held the key to uncovering the killer's plan. She quickly pulled up her e-reader once again, flipping through the pages of "Hamlet" until she found the scene in question.

"It's a warning," Elle explained, her voice filled with urgency. "The ghost of King Hamlet is cautioning against revenge and seeking justice outside of the law."

Tom furrowed his brow. "So you're saying that this killer sees himself as someone seeking revenge? And that his next victim might be someone he perceives as having wronged him?"

Elle nodded, her mind racing as she pieced together the puzzle. "Exactly. He believes that he is righteous in his quest for vengeance, and these quotes are his way of taunting us while also revealing bits of his twisted ideology."

Tom sighed heavily, leaning back in his chair. "This just keeps getting more complicated," he muttered.

Elle glanced at him, her eyes shining with determination. She looked back at the screen. And then paused. "Shit..."

"What?"

"Those symbols... they're not images. They're numbers."

"What language?"

Elle's eyes narrowed as she scrutinized the symbols on the screen. "It's a cipher," she said, her voice tinged with excitement. "But it's not one that I've encountered before."

Tom leaned in closer, his curiosity piqued. "Can you decipher it?"

Elle's fingers danced across her phone's keyboard as she quickly searched through her vast database of ciphers and encryption methods. After a few moments, she let out a triumphant gasp. "I've got it," she exclaimed. "It's a modified version of the Vigenère cipher."

Tom furrowed his brow, trying to make sense of the technical jargon. "What does that mean?"

Elle took a deep breath, her mind racing as she explained. "The Vigenère cipher is a method of encrypting text using a keyword. Each letter of the keyword determines the shift applied to the corresponding letter in the plaintext. But in this case, it seems like the killer has tweaked the method somehow."

"So how do we decrypt it?"

"We need to find the keyword," Elle said, her eyes fixed on the screen. "I just need to analyze the pattern of symbols and numbers and see if any recurring sequences stand out."

"So what's the keyword?"

She stared at her phone, frowning. "I... don't know."

"Try Shakespeare," he said.

She hesitated, doing some quick calculations, then she shook her head. "Too many letters."

"So how many letters does it need to be?"

"I don't know. But that one is too many."

"Try Hamlet."

She did, but then shook her head. "It's gibberish. Nothing."

"So... Macbeth?"

Again, she ran it through her software on her phone. "Nope."

"What about... murder?"

She glanced at him.

"What?"

"You want me to try *murder*?"

"Could be."

She didn't even plug it in this time, but rather rearranged the plaintext letters in her mind. "Nope."

"You didn't try."

"I did. I don't need my phone for that one. It doesn't work."

The two of them paused, both glaring at the screen now. "Well..." Tom said at last. "At least we know what type of cipher it is... What did you say it was called again?"

Elle sighed, her frustration mounting. "It's a modified Vigenère cipher," she replied, her voice tinged with exasperation. "But the keyword seems to elude us."

Tom rubbed his temples, deep in thought. "What if the keyword isn't related to Shakespeare at all? So we need to think outside the box," Tom added, his gaze fixed on the symbols and numbers on the screen. "We need to find a keyword that has personal significance to the killer."

Elle's mind raced through the details of the case—the victims, their backgrounds, any potential connections they might have had. And then it hit her.

"The victims," she said, her voice filled with certainty. "The common link between them is their love of acting and art... But I don't know if that helps us."

"So what now?" Tom said, glaring at the screen. "Just plug and play words?"

"We could... I mean, I may have to."

"Is that what you codebreakers do for a living?"

"Sometimes, yes," she replied. "I once heard a story from world war two where a British linguist cracked a German code using the word 'schadenfreude' because he knew that the Germans loved their compound words. Sometimes it's just about finding that unique insight into the mind of the person who created the code."

Tom nodded, his eyes flickering with a mix of anticipation and frustration. "Alright, let's give it a shot," he said, his voice filled with determination. "Think of words related to acting and art, but also something personal. Something that might resonate with the killer."

"Theater," she said quietly, her voice tinged with defeat before even trying it."

Tom looked at her, his eyes widening. "You think that could be it?"

"It's worth a try," she replied. "Theater is personal to the killer, given the victims' connection to acting and art. And it's also a word that holds significance in literature and Shakespeare."

Without hesitation, Elle began inputting the keyword into the decryption program on her phone. As she typed each letter, the symbols and numbers on the screen started to rearrange themselves...

And then...

"Nothing," she said, glaring.

"Shit... I thought that might be it," Tom said, frowning now.

"Maybe we're approaching this wrong," she said after a moment, her voice cutting across the hum of computers and the muted shuffle of papers. "We need someone who can look at this not just as a code, but as literature—someone who understands the psyche behind it."

"An expert?" Tom raised an eyebrow, the seed of curiosity planted amid the thorns of their dilemma.

"Exactly." Elle stood up, stretching her stiff muscles as her mind raced with possibilities. "Someone outside our circles, someone who's spent their life deciphering the intentions behind every penned word. A literary cryptographer as it were."

The suggestion hung in the air, a fragile lifeline in the vast ocean of their uncertainty. It was a long shot, but no longer could they afford to circle the drain of conventional tactics.

"Let's pitch it to the team," Tom said, rising alongside her. "What have we got to lose?"

"Only time," Elle answered, her resolve hardening. "And possibly our best chance at catching this killer before he writes another chapter in his twisted narrative."

With that, the two agents turned to go face their colleagues, ready to forge a new path in their hunt—a path that might finally lead them out of the darkness.

Elle leaned over the conference table, her fingers drumming a rhythm on the polished wood as she scanned the room. A constellation of furrowed brows and pursed lips surrounded her; the task force members exchanged helpless glances like lost ships signaling distress across a vast sea.

"Okay, spitball time," Elle declared, her voice lancing through the fog of defeat. "We need a name, someone who lives and breathes this stuff."

"Dr. Helena Graham," blurted out a junior agent from the corner, almost hesitantly. "She's pretty much the rock star of literary cryptography. I did my thesis on her work in grad school."

"Helena Graham?" Elle repeated, the name resonating with her own academic memories. She remembered reading Dr. Graham's papers, dense with knowledge yet thrilling like a detective novel, always leaving her hungry for more. The mention of Dr. Graham sparked a glimmer of hope in Elle's chest.

"Good. Very good," Tom murmured, leaning back in his chair with a thoughtful nod.

"Let's run with that." Elle's eyes were alight with determination now, a reflection of the fire that had been ignited by the mention of the seasoned cryptographer. "Graham could be our cipher key—the one who turns these nonsensical hieroglyphs into something we can actually use."

A moment later, Elle found herself sitting across from SAIC Harper in his office, its walls lined with commendations and a flag standing sentinel in the corner. His gaze was stern and expectant as he evaluated the agents before him.

"Dr. Helena Graham," Elle began without preamble, "her expertise in literary cryptography is unparalleled. She's not just a decoder; she understands the narrative elements of codes, the stories they tell. This killer... he's weaving a story for us, and she might just be the translator we desperately need."

Harper steepled his fingers, considering. He was a man of few words, but each one carried weight. His scrutiny felt like it could unravel a person's innermost thoughts, laying them bare on the table.

"Expanding our investigation to include a civilian consultant isn't standard procedure," Harper said slowly, his voice a low rumble. "But then again, nothing about this case has been."

"Sir, with all due respect, this killer is anything but standard," Elle insisted, her tone firm yet respectful. "We've hit a wall, and if there's any chance Dr. Graham can provide us with a fresh perspective, we need to take it."

Harper's eyes locked onto hers, searching. Elle met his gaze evenly.

"Alright, Agent Keen," Harper finally relented, a nod sealing his decision. "Bring in Dr. Graham. Let's see if she can shed some light on these dark messages."

"Thank you, sir," Elle responded, her voice steady despite the adrenaline coursing through her veins. She felt a surge of validation—this was the right move, she could feel it in her bones.

"Only problem," Tom said suddenly. "What if she's not available? If she's as well known as you say, I doubt she's just sitting around by a phone."

"You think she'd refuse an audience with the FBI?" Harper asked.

"No. I think she might reschedule," Tom said.

Elle bit her lower lip. Her partner was likely right. And the last thing they needed right now was to waste time.

Suddenly, an idea struck her. "I... I might know someone," she said. "Someone who's a colleague of Dr. Graham's. Who could get us a visit."

"Oh?" Tom said, quirking an eyebrow.

Harper was waving a hand as if to say *get on with it.* "Whatever works, Keen. Get moving."

"Yes, sir," she said quickly, pushing out of her chair and turning sharply towards the door.

Her phone was already in her hand, and she pressed a speed dial number, her anticipation already mounting.

CHAPTER EIGHTEEN

The sedan's engine hummed steadily, cutting through the silence of the evening hours as Elle Keen turned the steering wheel with a practiced hand. Beside her, Tom Wright adjusted his tailored suit, looking every inch the federal agent despite the late hour. They were en route to meet Dr. Helena Graham.

"Shaw says he can get us in before her schedule fills up," Elle said, sparing a glance at the GPS. It wasn't just a courtesy update; Professor Shaw, her old mentor, was the key to unlocking this next door. Their connection stretched back to university days, to lecture halls where she first learned to unravel the intricacies of cryptography under his tutelage.

"Good," Tom replied, his voice low and steady. "Every second counts." His gaze lingered on the passing scenery, but Elle knew his mind was churning through the case details just as hers was.

As they approached the rendezvous point, Elle felt a churn of anticipation in her gut. Shaw's involvement was necessary, yet it dredged up memories she often kept barricaded deep within her mind. He had been there after her parents' death, guiding her passion for codes into something tangible—a career that made sense of chaos.

The engine of the black SUV hummed steadily, cutting through the silent evening as it hurtled down the empty side street. Elle's eyes remained fixed on the blur of passing streetlights, her mind racing even faster than the vehicle.

"Helena Graham could be the key," Elle murmured, more to herself than to Tom, who merely nodded, his gaze never leaving the road.

"Let's hope she has the answers we need," he replied, his voice a low baritone that rumbled through the confines of the car.

The black vehicle sliced through the town's spacious arteries, a stark contrast to the pace of rush hour traffic in the heart of the city. Elle's fingers drummed against the leather-bound steering wheel, her eyes flicking between the road and the rearview mirror. A silence had settled between them since their departure, but as the buildings blurred past, Tom cleared his throat, signaling the end of their quiet.

"Did I ever tell you about my first day on patrol?" he asked, a lighthearted lilt in his voice that seemed almost out of place given the gravity of their mission.

Elle shook her head, the corner of her mouth lifting in a slight smile. "I'm guessing it wasn't a routine traffic stop."

"Far from it." Tom leaned back, his gaze distant. "It was a domestic disturbance call. We were rookies, fresh out of the academy, and I remember the adrenaline. We had no idea what we were walking into."

Elle's grip tightened on the steering wheel, her curiosity piqued. It was rare for Tom to share personal stories, and she knew that this one must hold some significance.

"We arrived at the scene," Tom continued, his voice tinged with a mixture of nostalgia and sadness. "The house was in complete disarray—broken furniture, shattered glass. And then we heard it—the sound of a baby crying from a back room."

Elle's heart clenched at the mention of an innocent child caught in the midst of chaos. She couldn't help but wonder how this related to their current case.

"We rushed towards the cries," Tom said, his eyes reflecting years of experience and emotion. "And there she was—a small, fragile baby girl, wrapped in a threadbare blanket, all alone in a world that had turned upside down. We managed to bring her to safety," Tom concluded softly, his gaze meeting Elle's. "That day taught me that behind every crime scene, behind every cipher we're trying to break, there's always someone who needs our help—someone who deserves their story to be told."

Elle nodded slowly, the weight of Tom's words sinking in. She knew that he was reminding her of their purpose as agents—to protect and

serve, to fight for justice and bring closure to those who had been victimized. It was a reminder that went beyond their current case, touching the very core of why she pursued this career in the first place.

"I understand," Elle said, her voice filled with determination. "We can't forget the human element amidst all the codes and ciphers. We're here to make a difference."

He blinked. "What the hell?"

"W-what?" she hesitated. Had she said something wrong?

He snorted in amusement.

"What?" she repeated, irritated now.

"Even when shooting the shit, you're still looking for a pattern."

"What do you mean? Did I miss the point?"

"The point is there is no point. I was just talking."

She stared at him, confused. "Wh... why?"

"Because we're friends, aren't we?"

"Not really."

"Partners, then," he said. "I was just chatting. Not everything has some hidden meaning."

She paused. "I mean... you were setting up a theme and everything. You were..." she trailed off and realized he was grinning now.

"Oh, haha. Funny."

He smirked. "Just playing there, Codebreaker. Your turn," he prodded after his laughter subsided. "Why law enforcement? Why not use your knack for puzzles in something...less dangerous?"

"Codes are truth," Elle stated simply, her eyes still on the road. "And truth matters. My parents..." She paused, the memory a shadow crossing her face. She didn't really want to tell him. But then again, Tom Wright was asking her.

It was a strange time to remember the woman back at the coffee shop. The digits she'd slipped Tom. She hesitated, wrinkling her nose. Then she released a long, pent-up sigh. "They believed in exposing lies. After they died, it felt like the only path that made sense."

"Huh... I see. Shit. Sorry about your parents."

"I told you before."

"Yeah. But I'm still sorry."

She nodded once, peering ahead towards the campus where they were due to meet with their expert, and their guide.

She didn't meet Tom's gaze for a moment, preferring a temporary calm and distance.

As they pulled into the university campus, a figure emerged from the shadow of the looming lecture hall—a silhouette Elle would recognize anywhere. Professor Shaw stood there, his posture rigid, the early morning light casting long shadows across his face. He had been waiting for them. Shaw had pale hair and a neat, trimmed goatee. He wore a suit two sizes too large for his thin, scarecrow frame. He often forgot to eat when delving into his studies.

"Elle," Shaw called out, his tone terse yet tinged with an undercurrent of warmth that was unusual for the no-nonsense, emotionally illiterate genius.

"Shaw," she responded, equally curt as she stepped out of the SUV. The air between them was electric, charged with unspoken words and a shared past.

"Still chasing shadows, I see," Shaw said, a hint of a smirk touching the corners of his lips. It was his way of showing affection, couched in intellectual banter.

"Only the ones that need catching," Elle shot back, her eyes locking onto his for a fleeting moment before breaking away. They understood each other too well, two minds that appreciated the pursuit of truth above all else, even when it hurt.

Tom observed the exchange silently, his presence a solid reassurance at her side. He knew the gravity of the journey they were on, the urgency that drove them forward to consult Dr. Helena Graham. This was no ordinary consultation; it was a race against time, a desperate bid to decode the twisted mind of a killer before another life was lost.

"Let's not keep Dr. Graham waiting," Elle said, her voice steady, betraying none of the turmoil she felt.

"Of course," Shaw replied, stepping aside to let them pass. "Good luck, Elle. You'll need it."

"Thanks again," she said.

"A favor for a friend," he replied. "But you owe me," he added. "I'm going to collect. I need help decoding an old

diary I stumbled upon, and I think you might be just the person for the job."

Elle raised an eyebrow at Shaw's request, intrigued by the prospect of unraveling yet another mystery. She nodded and shot him a wry smile.

"I suppose you've earned it," she said, her voice laced with a playful challenge. "But first, we have a killer to catch."

With that, Elle turned away from Shaw and headed towards the imposing lecture hall where Dr. Helena Graham awaited them. The doors creaked open, revealing a dimly lit corridor lined with posters of past academic conferences, their faded colors peeling at the edges. As Elle and Tom followed the path towards Dr. Graham's office, a sense of anticipation settled over them like a heavy fog.

When they reached the door, Elle paused for a moment to gather herself. She took a deep breath, feeling the weight of responsibility settle on her shoulders. The fate of future victims depended on what they would uncover within these cryptic messages.

With a quick glance at Tom, who offered an encouraging nod, Elle approached the heavy oak door. She knocked lightly, then pushed it open. Inside, the air was thick with the musk of old paper and the metallic tang of machine oil. Shelves reached up to the ceiling, each row teeming with textbooks that ranged from ancient languages to modern computational theory. Desks were strewn with papers, cipher wheels, and mechanical decoders that clicked and whirred softly, like dormant creatures waiting to spring to life at their master's touch.

"Quite the cryptographer's den," Elle remarked, her eyes scanning the organized chaos. She could almost feel the pulse of Dr. Graham's intellect within these walls—a kindred spirit dedicated to peeling back layers of obfuscation, revealing the stark bones of reality beneath.

"Let's hope she can shed some light on our killer's dark obsessions," Tom said, his voice echoing slightly in the vast room.

Elle nodded, the weight of their task settling over her once again. Here, amongst the silent sentinels of knowledge, they might just find the key they were looking for.

Finally, Elle's gaze landed on a single figure sitting in a leather chair by an electric fireplace. Columns of stacked books surrounded the chair's occupant.

Dr. Graham's gaze met theirs from across the room, her eyes reflecting the same intensity that Elle recognized in her own when piecing together a particularly challenging cipher. Graham had pale hair, and she wore

a pair of wire-framed glasses that perched delicately on the bridge of her nose. She was petite, but held an air of authority that demanded respect. As Elle and Tom approached, Dr. Graham rose gracefully from her chair, the books whispering in protest as she disrupted their arrangement.

"Agent Keen, Agent Wright," Dr. Graham greeted them with a warm smile. "I've been expecting you." Her voice was melodic, carrying a sense of wisdom and experience.

Elle couldn't help but feel a surge of relief at the professor's calm presence. It was a balm to her racing thoughts and reminded her that they were not alone in this intricate dance with the killer. She found herself eager to share their findings and seek Dr. Graham's expertise.

"Thank you for seeing us on such short notice, Dr. Graham," Tom said, extending his hand in greeting.

She accepted it graciously before motioning for them to sit in the two armchairs that faced her desk. Elle took in her surroundings once more, noticing how the room seemed to have a life of its own—each book whispering secrets from the shelves while old world maps adorned the walls, hinting at uncharted territories waiting to be explored.

As they settled into their seats, Dr. Graham's gaze shifted between them both, curiosity shining in her eyes. "Tell me about your investigation so far," she prompted, her voice filled with genuine interest. "Dr. Shaw says a lot of good things about you, Elle." She paused. "And for Shaw, that's tantamount to a rave review." She smiled, and Elle returned the gesture.

"Same of you," Elle said quickly. Shaw was standing in the door, watching his phone. Likely engaged in his own work now that his services had already been rendered. She bit back a chuckle at the sight of the scrawny professor wearing such a concentrated look while standing in a doorway.

She returned her attention to Graham.

"I've been looking at the photos you sent ahead," Graham replied, pointing to some laminates sitting on her desk.

"And?" Tom asked.

He sat, uninvited, into one of the leather chairs facing the stacks of books. Graham sat as well, gesturing for Elle to take the stool by the desk, which she did.

"Most code-makers who delve into complexity do so out of an inherent need to conceal," Dr. Graham continued, tapping a pen against a thick textbook on cryptanalysis. "But there's more—it's about control, a power play. They're puppeteers who delight in watching others struggle to untangle their web."

"Like a superiority complex?" Elle asked, recalling the meticulous ciphers left at each crime scene by the killer.

"Exactly," Dr. Graham affirmed. "And in our killer's case, it's not just about being superior. It's a challenge—a dare to law enforcement, a taunt that screams 'catch me if you can.'"

Tom nodded slowly, processing the information. "So, we're dealing with someone who gets off on the chase as much as the crime."

"Quite so," Dr. Graham said, her eyes sharpening. "Now, let's discuss literary cryptography. Codes woven through classic literature."

She gestured towards a wall lined with books that seemed to whisper secrets accumulated over centuries. Pulling down a well-worn copy of Dante's "Inferno," Dr. Graham flipped through the pages until she found the passage she sought.

"Consider this," she said, pointing to a stanza in the epic poem. "The layers of meaning within these lines have been debated for ages. Our killer uses similar methods—embedding messages within messages. The surface text may tell one story, but beneath lies another, far more personal."

"Personal how?" Elle inquired, her interest piqued.

"Perhaps it's autobiographical or relates to a vendetta," Dr. Graham speculated. "It could also be a form of confession, camouflaged within the grandeur of prose. The key lies in identifying which texts resonate with the killer and why."

"Could this be a way to anticipate his next move?" Tom asked, his brow furrowed in thought.

"Potentially," Dr. Graham replied, meeting Tom's gaze with a nod of agreement. "By decoding his literary choices, you may uncover his motivations, his past... perhaps even his future targets."

"He likes Shakespeare," Tom said. "And the code is actually a type of... What was it again? Vignette... no. Something cipher? A modified..." he wrinkled his nose, glancing at Elle.

She rolled her eyes, but cut back the expression. Not everyone spent their lives with heads buried in books, and she needed to remember that. She said, "It's a type of modified vigenère cipher. It's a polyalphabetic substitution cipher that uses a keyword to encrypt and decrypt the message. Each letter of the keyword corresponds to a different alphabet, making it harder to crack."

Dr. Graham's eyes sparkled with admiration as she looked at Elle. "Impressive," she said. "You have quite the command over cryptography."

Elle shrugged, not one for compliments. "It's just a skill I picked up along the way."

"But a skill that could prove vital in deciphering our killer's messages," Dr. Graham pointed out. "If we can identify the literary sources he draws from, we might be able to anticipate his next move or even gain insight into his psyche."

Elle leaned forward, her curiosity getting the better of her. "Do you have any ideas on where we should start looking?"

Dr. Graham nodded, her fingers tapping lightly on the desk. "Given his affinity for Shakespeare, we could begin by examining plays like 'Macbeth' or 'Richard III.' These are known for their themes of ambition, power struggles, and manipulation—qualities that seem to align with our killer's profile."

Tom leaned back in his chair, drumming his fingers thoughtfully on the armrest. "So we're hunting for a modern-day Macbeth? That's what we thought. He used Macbeth twice in the message he sent to us."

"Perhaps," Dr. Graham replied. "But we must also consider other classics that delve into similar themes. Literature is vast, and our killer could draw inspiration from a wide range of sources."

Elle's mind raced with possibilities as she considered the countless books lining Dr. Graham's office walls. "I'm guessing you won't have something for us overnight?"

"What I'm willing to do," Graham said, "Is to put together a list. Keywords. The most likely words that fit thematically as well as cryptographically. I'll happily send these keywords your way once I've populated the list. It should be plug and play, then, for you to run them through an algorithm and determine if

they match any of the encoded messages you've received so far."

Elle's eyes lit up at the offer. "That would be incredibly helpful, Dr. Graham. Thank you."

Dr. Graham smiled warmly. "Think nothing of it, my dear. I've always been fascinated by the intersection of literature and cryptography. And if I can assist in bringing this killer to justice, then it would be my honor."

As they continued discussing potential literary sources and keywords, Elle's phone buzzed with an incoming call. Elle's phone vibrated against the heavy silence that had settled in the room, a violent buzz that seemed to echo off the walls lined with books. She glanced at the screen and saw that it was her boss, Special Agent In Charge Leonard Harper.

"Excuse me for a moment," she said, stepping away from the desk. She answered the call and brought the phone to her ear.

"Keen," she answered, her voice steady despite the quickening pulse at her temple.

"Agent Keen, this is Harper. Where the hell are you now?"

She frowned. "With Graham."

"Yeah, well, we've got another one. Victim's name is Holly Jensen according to a caller who reported it. I need you on-site, now."

The words hit Elle like a physical blow, her breath caught somewhere between her chest and throat. Her eyes darted to Tom, who was watching with an intensity that mirrored the gravity of the moment.

"Address?" Elle managed to ask, mentally preparing to shift gears from scholarly pursuit to the grim reality of their chase.

"Texting it to you. Time is of the essence."

"Understood." Elle ended the call, the digital beep sounding far too mundane for the chaos it heralded.

"Another victim," she said, turning back to Dr. Graham and Tom, her face pale but composed. "Holly Jensen. We have to go—now."

Dr. Graham's eyes, usually brimming with academic curiosity, now reflected a deep concern. "Be careful," she advised, her voice tinged with something akin to maternal worry.

Elle nodded briskly, her mind already racing through the logistics of reaching the crime scene. The realization that they were dealing with a serial killer who operated at a rapid pace—a predator who lurked in the shadows of their own data, striking out with brutal precision—sent a shiver down her spine. How many more would he claim? Fear coursed through her veins, not for her own safety, but for the innocents caught in the crosshairs of a madman's game.

"Let's move," Elle commanded, her tone leaving no room for hesitation as she strode towards the door. Tom was right behind her, his presence a silent vow of support.

She paused. "Any chance you can try and overnight that list, Dr. Graham?"

"Y-yes!" The literary expert said quickly. "I'll do my best!"

Elle nodded in gratitude.

As they exited Dr. Graham's office, Elle's thoughts were a maelstrom of code sequences and cryptic messages, but above all, there was the haunting image of Holly Jensen—a name now etched into the case file of their relentless pursuit. The weight of responsibility bore down on her shoulders; every second they delayed was a concession to the killer's grim timetable.

"Keen, we'll catch this guy," Tom reassured her as they descended the stairs, his words cutting through the fog of her apprehension.

"Hope is not a strategy," Elle replied sharply, her walnut hair streaking behind her like a battle flag. But in her heart, she clung to that hope, fragile and defiant, as they raced against the ticking clock of a killer's design.

The engine of the unmarked SUV roared to life, a beast awakened by urgency. Elle jammed the key into the ignition, her movements practiced and precise. They were already threading through the labyrinthine streets of the city, the office of Dr. Graham shrinking into the distance behind them.

"GPS says fifteen minutes to the crime scene," Tom said, his voice steady despite the tension that knitted his brow. His fingers flew over the small screen, plotting their course with swift taps.

"Make it ten," Elle countered, her hands gripping the steering wheel as she navigated the traffic with an expert's anticipation. Buildings blurred past them, the urban landscape a mere backdrop to their mission. The logical sequence of their path was like a code in itself—one Elle could decipher with her eyes closed.

"Elle, remember breathing? It's that thing you're forgetting to do right now," Tom joked, attempting to lighten the mood, even as his eyes remained vigilant, scanning for the quickest route.

"Breath is a luxury we don't have, Tom," she snapped back, her foot pressing harder against the accelerator. The car responded eagerly, cutting through the city's arteries like a blade.

They swung onto a narrower street, the GPS marking their progress with every tick of the clock. The sedan's tires screeched in protest as Elle pushed the vehicle to its limits, a symphony of urgency that screamed through the concrete jungle.

"Left up ahead!" Tom directed, pointing to an alley that shaved precious seconds off their journey. Elle took the turn on two wheels, the g-force pressing them into their seats.

"Nice move," he grunted, the corner of his mouth lifting in reluctant admiration. "Next right, then straight to the end," Tom said as they neared their destination. The crackling static of the police radio melded with the cacophony of sirens in the near distance, heralding their approach.

"Got it." Elle's jaw set, the lines of her face hardening with resolve. She made the turn, the scene unfolding before them: red and blue lights painting the night, officers moving with purpose, and the grim tapestry of crime scene tape.

"Go, I'll park," Tom offered, already undoing his seatbelt as Elle brought the car to a halt at the edge of the chaos.

"Thanks." Elle didn't wait for the vehicle to fully stop before she was out, sprinting towards the epicenter of activity, her badge glinting under the harsh lights.

CHAPTER NINETEEN

Elle stared at the body under the tarp in the middle of the park. She frowned, frozen in place. A couple of cops lingered nearby, muttering to each other. An open book lay by the outstretched hand of the victim... A cold, rigid hand.

Very rigid. She stared.

And then she scowled. "Agent," one of the cops said, noting her glare.

She marched towards the body under the tarp, moving swiftly.

"Agent!" one of the cops said, trying to reach out. "Forensics hasn't come through yet.

But she kicked away the book, *Shakespeare's Classics.*

And yanked the tarp back.

"This is your victim?" she demanded, rounding on the cop and pointing an accusing finger.

It was a mannequin.

"Dammit!" Elle muttered under her breath, resisting the urge to kick the mannequin for deceiving her. She turned to face the cop who had failed to give her accurate details about the crime scene.

"What's the meaning of this?" she snapped, her voice laced with annoyance. "Why was I called here for a mannequin?"

The cop shifted uncomfortably, his eyes darting away from Elle's piercing gaze. "I... I'm sorry, Agent Keen," he stammered. "We received an anonymous tip claiming there was a body in the park. We didn't realize it was a mannequin. Anonymous tip gave us the name. Made up, I guess."

Elle's jaw clenched as she fought to regain her composure. She had a reputation for being brusque, but she knew that berating the officer wouldn't solve anything.

"Find out who gave you that tip," she ordered, her voice firm but controlled. "I want their name, and I want it now."

The cop nodded meekly and scurried off to follow Elle's command while she stood there, contemplating her next move. It was clear to her that someone had intentionally misled law enforcement, wasting their time and resources.

But the book... Shakespeare. A coincidence?

No... No, it wasn't. Her eyes narrowed, and she dropped to a knee, opening the book. She paused.

It was addressed to her.

To my dearest Tom and Elle.

But he'd spelt it *TomandElle.* As if it were one word. She frowned, standing slowly. She could hear Tom's footsteps behind her.

"What the hell is that?" Tom called out, his voice laced with disgust.

But she shook her head, her mind racing. "Elle?" he called.

She turned to face him. "I think... I think this is our keyword," she murmured.

"What?"

"He wants us to find him. He wants the notoriety. He's taunting us."

"What's the keyword?"

She showed him the first page of the book.

"He's giving it to us? He knows our names?"

"Apparently."

"Shit," Tom said.

But Elle was already hastily pulling out her phone to find the cipher. If the keyword was TomandElle, then she'd be able to find how to replace the other letters in the messages he'd left at the crime scenes. He'd been one step ahead... She was getting tired of being so far behind.

As her fingers trembled, and she stood in the cold, by the mannequin laying under the blue tarp, she entered the letters on her phone, running the algorithimic software she'd coded herself.

And then a hit.

She stared.

"Well?" Tom asked.

"It's right. It's the keyword."

"What does it say?" he asked, excitedly.

She froze in place, eyes canning rapidly. And then, in a whisper, she murmured, "*The next theatrical release is my own.*"

She blinked... paused, then cursed. "He's going to kill himself, Tom... But... But he'll take down others. People like this want to go out in a blaze of glory."

"Where? Does it say where?"

"No!" she said, cursing.

She paced back and forth, and then her eyes widened. "Wait!" she said suddenly.

"What?"

"I... I think... he says theatrical release. That's not a stage play term. That's a movie theater term."

"You think he's at a movie theater?"

"Yes... yes, very possible. But it would be a high brow type. Not a mainstream theater."

"So... we need to find some snobby movie theater nearby? Right? He can't be far? How many of those are there?"

She was already searching on her phone. She took a few moments, narrowing the results based on showings. A few art-house theaters. Some that showed foreign flicks... and then she clicked her fingers. "It would be prestigious. High end."

"So?"

"There's two," she said, looking up sharply.

He grimaced. "You're sure?"

"As sure as I can be."

"You think he's going to kill everyone in a theater?"

"And then himself, yes," she said urgently. "We need to split up. Tom! You're going to this one," she shoved her phone so he could read. "Hurry!"

"I need to borrow your car!" she yelled as she rounded to the sulking officer she'd tongue-lashed earlier. She hastened towards him, hand-outstretched, heart pumping wildly.

***

The gray fingers of evening clawed at the horizon, donning the night's veil as Elle parked her borrowed cruise across from the weathered facade of the old theater. It loomed—brooding and unwelcoming—as if harboring secrets within its crumbling walls. She sat for a moment, the engine's soft purr dying into silence, her breath visible in the cool air of the early morning.

The theater in question was old. As old as any she'd seen. It didn't even have a name, as most of the letters had peeled off, but online, the place was called *Picture House Remedies.*

Pretentious name, pretentious content. Check. Check.

Was she going to find the killer here, though?

She frowned, approaching the theater. Tom had already reached his location. Her phone buzzed and she spotted his most recent update. "Negative. No one here. Stay safe. I'm on my way."

She pocketed her phone.

The second theater was cleared. So what if she was making a mistake? What if this was all for naught?

She shook her head, frowning as her gaze swept side to side.

What was it she had missed in all of this? A few cars were parked in the theater's lot. An idea struck her. Hastily, she pulled out her phone, running the license plates quickly.

The first car belonged to a

young couple who had tickets to a late-night showing of an avant-garde French film. Nothing suspicious there. The second car, however, sent a chill down Elle's spine. It belonged to a man named Arthur Drescher, a known recluse who had a history of mental health issues. But no... no, he was wheelchair-bound.

And then she spotted the largest car in the lot. A big, gleaming truck, intended to draw the eye.

The owner was a man named Adam Stone.

She frowned, scanning through information on the man. A librarian... She stared. Adam had hooded eyes and sallow features. He looked bored as he stared out from his DMV photo.

Adam Stone's mother had some google searches. She'd been a failed novelist, by the look of things, judging from the number of reviews on her books.

She'd passed away only two months ago...

Right around when the murders had started.

A cold, creeping sensation crawled up Elle's spine.

"Adam?" she asked, staring. Hardly the theater aficionado she'd first assumed. But maybe that was the point. He was the son of an author, not a director... He was a... librarian? Someone who would have access to books. Who knew literature as his trade.

She looked through info on the next two cars, just in case, her heart pounding.

Then her attention returned to the small theater.

The building exuded an aura of neglect, windows boarded up, and ivy climbing the walls like veins on a corpse. Its presence was a disquieting whisper in the otherwise hushed neighborhood, as if it harbored secrets too dark for daylight to uncover. Elle's resolve steeled her spine, but that did not stop the involuntary shiver that trailed down it as she neared the entrance.

With a final glance over her shoulder, Elle reached for the door handle, the metal cold and unyielding beneath her touch. She pulled with steady force, and the door groaned open on neglected hinges, protesting the disturbance. A waft of musty air rushed to greet her, laden with the scent of decayed leather and paper—the smell of a literary tomb.

She stepped across the threshold, her eyes taking a moment to adjust to the dimness within.

Off to the right, she spotted the theater. A small room, the doors propped open. Figures inside were staring at a large screen on the wall, chatting to each other as they waited for their feature to start.

"Everyone out!" she called, her eyes scanning for Adam Stone, or anyone else who might be a threat. "Hey, all of you! FBI! Get out of here, now!"

Figures turned to look at her, alarmed.

Elle's heart hammered against her chest as the patrons slowly filed out, confusion etched across their faces. She scanned the gathering, searching for any sign of Adam Stone or any suspicious behavior. Her eyes landed on a man standing near the back of the theater, his hands tucked into the pockets of his trench coat. But when she looked closer, she realized it was a large woman who looked flustered as she tried to usher a petulant teenager out the exit door.

A few figures tried to stop, to question her, but she waved them away.

Once the theater was empty, she continued to scan for any signs of the librarian... Adam Stone...

Did she really think he was their guy?

For now, she'd cleared the theater. She had names due to license plates.

She needed to clear the building. She turned away, moving towards a stairase across from the large double doors of the entrance.

With each cautious step, Elle's boots echoed softly against the ancient wood of the theater's floor. The creaking sounded like strained whispers in the oppressive silence, betraying her presence to the unseen watcher she knew lurked within. She paused, listening for a response, but was met only by the quiet, as if the building itself were holding its breath.

The shadowy corners of the vast hall at the top of the stairs seemed to pulse with potential menace. Adam could be anywhere, his presence like a specter haunting the long-forgotten aisles of this literary crypt. Elle's heart thrummed a relentless rhythm, yet her hands were steady—a dichotomy born from years of mastering control in chaos.

She clicked on her flashlight, the beam slicing through the darkness ahead. As she moved it left to right, dust motes danced in the artificial daybreak before settling back into their undisturbed slumber. Her finger rested near the trigger of her gun, a silent promise that she would not be taken by surprise.

A bookcase lined the hall at the top of the theater. She frowned. Did someone live here? Adam? The light trembled over spines of books, titles embossed in gold and faded letters, genres spanning from romantic poetry to treatises on human psychology. They were relics, witnesses to an era when they were cradled by hands eager for knowledge, now reduced to mere spectators.

Her breathing was controlled, shallow enough to keep silent, yet deep enough to sustain the adrenaline-fueled vigilance that coursed through her veins. Each breath felt like an intrusion on the sacred stillness, every heartbeat a thunderous drumroll that might summon the predator from his hiding place.

Elle's flashlight beam steadied on an alcove, where a plush armchair sat under the focused circle of a brass reading lamp. The seat cushion bore the imprint of recent occupancy, the only place amidst the upstair's chaos that seemed to cradle a lingering human touch. A discarded tumbler, with its dregs of dark liquid, rested on the small table beside it. This was his nest, she realized, the epicenter.

And there, sitting by the chair... a rifle. A semi-automatic rifle.

The weapon he'd been intending to use.

Shit. She sent out a quick distress call on the radio, wordless, but entering the code for backup.

She took the rifle in hand, unchambered the rounds, and tossed the magazine aside. Her own sidearm was now gripped tightly.

She tried not to think what might have happened to the people downstairs if she hadn't shown up in time.

Cautiously, she edged forward, her steps muted against the threadbare carpet that adorned the floor of the secluded spot. The air felt different here—denser, as if soaked with the residue of contemplation and madness. Elle's intellect, which so often insulated her from emotion, now throbbed with palpable tension. She recognized it for what it was—a prelude to confrontation—and allowed herself to embrace the surge of instinctual readiness.

The sudden sound of movement shattered the quietude like the crack of a spine of an over-opened book.

"What are you doing here?" A soft, lilting voice spoke.

It was like the aged creaking of hinges. The voice extended to meet her, sending goosebumps up her spine.

She met the gaunt man's gaze. He was pale. So very, very pale. His eyes set deep in his skull. His face was smooth, though, trimmed. And he wore an expensive outfit, consisting of

a tailored suit that seemed out of place in this decaying theater. His silver tie glimmered under the muted light, reflecting hints of a sinister charm.

Elle's grip tightened around her weapon, her finger inching towards the trigger. "Adam? Is that you?" she demanded, her voice steady despite the adrenaline surging through her veins.

Adam Stone grinned, his lips parting to reveal a row of perfectly white teeth. "Ah, Agent Keen," he said, his voice dripping with an unsettling sweetness. "I've been expecting you."

Elle's mind raced, trying to piece together the fragments of information she had about Adam Stone. He was a former librarian. But there was more to him than met the eye.

He was staring at her, so calm. Why was he so damn calm?

Adam's gaze did not waver, his eyes tracking her with a predator's precision. Elle felt the weight of his attention like a physical force, pressing against her with the gravity of all the stories that surrounded them—tales of intrigue and betrayal that paled in comparison to the reality they were living. Her hand finally clasped the grip of her firearm, the familiarity of its contour grounding her in the moment.

The dim light cast shadows across Adam's face, but it could not obscure the intensity of his stare nor the slight curl of his lip that hinted at a twisted satisfaction. In the stillness, Elle tasted the metallic tang of adrenaline, her senses heightened as if she were deciphering the most complex cipher.

"Adam," Elle began, her voice steady, betraying none of the torrential emotions churning within. "You've made your mark on the world, though not as you intended." She gestured slightly toward the shelves lined with literary classics, each spine a silent witness to the drama unfolding between them. "But this... these recreations of yours, they are abominations, not homages."

Her words were deliberate, each one chosen and placed with the same precision she used when piecing together the fragments of coded messages. She watched him closely, not just his face but his body language, the minutiae that betrayed one's true intent. It was a game of cat and mouse, only the roles of predator and prey were not so clearly defined.

She wanted a confession. A final confirmation of what seemed so clear now.

"Your fascination with literature is profound," she continued, allowing the faintest hint of fascination to color her tone, acknowledging the intellect behind the madness. "Shakespeare, Poe, Christie—they spoke of death, yes, but there was always a reason, a lesson within the tragedy. What lesson do you believe you're teaching with your..." She paused, searching for the word that would strike a chord within him. "...interpretations?"

Adam's lips curled into a semblance of a smile, the kind that never reached his eyes. "You of all people should understand, Agent Keen," he said, his voice as smooth as the leather bindings on the rare editions that surrounded them. "The world is full of pretenders—people who claim to respect the artistry of words but lack any true comprehension."

Elle felt a wave of dread wash over her as he spoke so casually of his crimes. His nonchalance in the face of such horror was more unsettling than any show of anger could have been. Yet she stood unwavering, her resolve as firm as the conviction that had led her to this moment.

"Adam," Elle began, her tone measured, letting the silence between her words hang heavy in the air, "do you remember the first story that ever truly moved you? The one that made you feel... understood?"

He narrowed his eyes, his guard momentarily slipping as he searched her face for signs of mockery. But he found none—only genuine curiosity.

"Of course," he replied after a beat, his voice quieter now. "It was a revelation."

"Then isn't it tragic," she pressed on, each word carefully chosen, "to think that the same stories that once offered solace are now being used to justify such... brutality?"

Elle watched as Adam's stoicism wavered, his adamantine facade cracking just enough to let her see the uncertainty flicker within the depths of his gaze. She knew then that she had struck a nerve.

"Brutality?" Adam countered, though his voice lacked its earlier conviction. "I am merely an instrument, ensuring that the sanctity of these works is not defiled by those unworthy of their messages."

"But who decides worthiness?" Elle challenged softly, stepping forward. Her movement was not aggressive, but it held purpose. She needed to corral him. To keep him talking.

Her gun was trained on him, but he didn't seem to care.

Elle inched nearer, the dim light casting shadows across her determined features. "Your mother," she said, her tone shifting to something more pointed, "the novelist who never saw success—the world never deemed her writings worthy." She watched Adam's face carefully, noting the twitch in his jaw, the slight narrowing of his eyes. "She wrote her own ending, didn't she?"

Adam's stance stiffened, and the air around them seemed to thicken with unspoken truths. Elle had struck a nerve; she could see it in the way his hands clenched and unclenched at his sides.

"Does your crusade honor her memory, Adam?" Elle pressed on, her voice steady but probing. She needed him off balanace. Needed to keep him here until backup arrived.

Why the hell was he *so damn calm*?

"Enough!" The word erupted from Adam like a thunderclap, slicing through the hush of the library. His face, normally so composed, now betrayed a tumult of emotions roiling just beneath the surface.

Elle's pulse quickened, but her gaze remained locked on him, unyielding. "Laura Davis, Sarah Mason," she continued methodically, as if reciting lines from one of the very books that surrounded them. "They were readers, lovers of words just like she was. But you chose them, Adam. You played judge, jury... executioner."

The mention of his victims' names hung between them, a specter that neither could ignore. With each syllable, Elle painted a picture of their lives, of the stories they would never get to tell because of him. She wielded her knowledge like a weapon, each fact a calculated thrust aimed to weaken his defenses.

"Tell me about Laura," Elle demanded softly, yet with an edge of steel in her voice. "And Rebecca. Were they truly unworthy? Or were they simply convenient targets for your misplaced vengeance?"

Adam's breaths came heavier now, his composure slipping like sand through fingers. Elle knew she was close, close to breaking the façade, close to unraveling the enigma of Adam Stone. In the musty silence of the old theater, it was not just a confrontation—it was a battle for the final truth.

Adam's eyes, once the still surface of a frozen lake, now churned with stormy rage. The dusty air seemed to thicken as his hands clenched into fists at his sides. Elle watched him, every muscle coiled and ready, though her face betrayed none of her anticipation.

"Enough!" Adam's voice, a blade drawn in desperation, cut through the silence. It was the sound of a cornered animal snarling against inevitable capture.

Then, he moved—a swift, sudden blur of motion.

He had something in his hand. A phone. He pressed something. A click. A beeping sound.

Her eyes widened.
The place was rigged.
She flung herself to the side, lunging at the bookcase for cover.
Then the loud *BOOOOM!*

CHAPTER TWENTY

The blast ripped through the theater's second floor, shattering windows and sending debris flying in all directions. Elle felt a searing pain in her side as she collided with the bookcase, shielding herself from the worst of the explosion. Dust filled the air, obscuring her vision and filling her lungs.

Coughing and gasping for breath, Elle fought through the chaos, desperately searching for any sign of Adam amidst the wreckage. She could hear sirens in the distance, growing closer with each passing second. Backup would be here soon, but time was running out.

Using every ounce of strength she had left, Elle pushed herself up from the floor and staggered forward. The scene was one of devastation—burnt books scattered like ashes, splintered wood jutting out from broken shelves. But there was no sign of Adam.

She stumbled towards where she last saw him, her mind racing to piece together what had just happened. Had he managed to escape? Or was he buried beneath the destruction he had caused?

As Elle made her way through the wreckage, her foot caught on something—a tattered page torn from a book.

And then, a flicker of movement out of the corner of her eye.

She spun around just in time.

Adam lunged towards Elle, propelled by the fury she had stoked within him. Burning books, ancient and forgotten, rained down around them as his body collided with the shelves in his frenzied assault.

Elle's heart leaped into her throat, her body reacting a split-second slower than her mind. She stumbled backward, her training surfacing from the depths of her ingrained instincts. Spinning away, she narrowly evaded his outstretched grasp, her breaths shallow bursts in the charged atmosphere.

She pivoted on her heel, watching Adam's momentum carry him past her. His breath was ragged, his movements uncontrolled—a stark contrast to the calculated precision that had marked his crimes.

The room spun with dislodged literature, the words of countless authors suspended in the air as if witnessing the culmination of their darkest narratives. Elle ducked another wild swing, feeling the whoosh of air as it passed harmlessly inches from her face.

As his hand lashed out again, aiming for her throat, Elle's own hand shot up in defense, redirecting the force of his attack. The move was fluid, an echo of countless hours spent in practice sessions, where the line between survival and defeat was drawn in sweat on gym mats.

Her other hand found its way to his wrist, gripping firmly, applying pressure to a nerve she knew well. Adam's face contorted in pain, his advance momentarily halted as if he had forgotten that she, too, was versed in the language of violence.

Adam's next punch came fast, a blur of motion aimed to incapacitate. Yet Elle was swifter, her body instinctively ducking as the fist whistled over her head, grazing the loose strands of her hair that had escaped her ponytail.

She nearly stumbled, her foot breaking through the floor, weakened by the explosion. A creaking sound and crashing noise suggest part of the staircase behind her had fallen.

He'd rigged the theater.

Again, she pictured all those innocents who'd been led away.

With the agility of a panther, she sidestepped another wild blow, her keen eyes reading his movements like the pages of an open book. The irony wasn't lost on her—the killer who staged his crimes as literary tableaus now faltering in his own narrative. She feinted left and struck right, her knuckles connecting with Adam's rib cage, eliciting a grunt that echoed off the ornate ceilings of the library.

A fierce uppercut from Adam grazed Elle's jaw, sending a jolt of pain through her skull. Her vision blurred momentarily, but her resolve did not waver.

Gritting her teeth, she seized the moment when Adam's guard dropped ever so slightly. With a swift move born from countless drills, she twisted his arm behind his back, forcing him to drop the makeshift weapon he had snatched from a nearby table—a letter opener masquerading as a dagger in his desperate grasp.

Using her momentum, Elle delivered a powerful blow to the side of his knee, bringing the larger man crashing down like a felled oak. The thud of his body hitting the floor sent a cloud of dust swirling into the air, motes dancing like tiny specters in the beam of her flashlight.

She wasted no time, her hands working with practiced efficiency to restrain him with handcuffs she always carried, a cold metal promise of justice. His face pressed against the worn carpet, Adam's breaths came out in ragged gasps, mirroring Elle's own labored breathing. She stood up, towering over the man who thought himself the arbiter of life and death.

"Rehearsal is over," she whispered, her voice steady despite the adrenaline that coursed through her veins. The theater, once again, fell eerily silent, save for the echo of their heavy breathing and the distant sound of sirens approaching, a herald of the endgame.

CHAPTER TWENTY ONE

Elle ran around the track at her local gym again... and again... she kept picturing the innocent lives filtering out of the theater. She kept picturing the figures fleeing the darkness.

Then the explosion.

It still echoed in her ears.

Adam had wept as they'd arrested him.

She frowned, circling the track again, arms pumping like pistons.

The familiar rhythm of her footsteps helped calm her racing thoughts, grounding her in the present moment. But no matter how many laps she ran, she couldn't escape the haunting memories of that night at the theater. The faces of the innocent victims flickered in her mind like fragments of a shattered mirror, reflecting the pain and fear they had experienced.

As Elle sprinted around the track, her mind delved into the depths of Adam's motives.

His own mother died. His own life amounting to little...

She hated defining success in life as success in career, but Adam accomplished neither. He'd treated people like props for his own infamy.

She'd asked Harper to leave his name out of the report. But Harper hadn't thought it possible. And now she was here, blowing off steam.

Suddenly, footsteps echoed beside her. She glanced over to see Tom running alongside.

She picked up her pace, frowning.

"Hey there, codebreaker," Tom said, easily. It was as if he were simply out for a stroll in the park. Wearing sweats and a t-shirt, she hardly recognized her usually suit-clad partner.

"I told Leo," she snapped, breathing heavily and hating her lungs for this show of weakness, "But I need to be alone."

"Sure... yeah... sure," he said. "Just... thought you might want this."

He handed her a piece of paper.

She didn't slow at first. But as he kept pace, the paper crinkling as they both ran, she finally paused, turning to him, exasperated.

"What is this?" she demanded.

He stopped, too, looking sheepishly at her.

"Well," he said slowly. "It's what we talked about in the car."

"What?"

"Your... parents," he said.

She froze as if she'd been slapped. "You went digging into my parents' death?"

He winced. "I was worried you'd react this way."

"Tom, what the hell? You had no right!"

She was breathing heavily, sweating, and now glaring intently at her partner, anger bubbling up.

"I know, Elle," Tom began, his voice filled with remorse. "I shouldn't have done it without your permission. But I couldn't help myself. I saw how much it still haunted you."

"Who the hell said it hunated me?"

"Er, you?"

"I didn't say that."

He rubbed sheepishly at the back of his head. "Well... damn. I thought that maybe if I could find something, anything, it could bring you some closure."

Elle's anger softened slightly as she listened to Tom's explanation. She understood his intentions, even if his actions were misguided. Taking a deep breath, she reached out and snatched the crumpled piece of paper from his hand.

"What did you find?" she asked, her voice a mixture of curiosity and irritation.

Tom hesitated for a moment before answering. "It's a letter," he said. "A letter that your parents wrote just days before they died."

Elle's heart skipped a beat at the mention of the letter. "Wh-what?"

He nodded.

She frowned. "I was never told about any letter."

"Yeah... well, that was because it was in evidence last time you checked the case files. It was only released a few months ago. Custodian did some house cleaning of evidence lockers. This was found along with some cash. Someone had mis-logged it."

He was studying her closely, as if hopeful she wasn't still mad at him.

She stared, stunned,

"W-what?"

"Yeah," he said hurriedly. "It's... like I said."

She let out a slow, shaking breath. "I..." she trailed off. "You're sure?"

"Yeah. You know how old cases are. It wasn't the same transmission of evidence we have now."

"What's the letter say?"

"I didn't read it," he said hurriedly. "Didn't want to..."

"Invade my privacy?"

He winced. "Sorry," he muttered.

But she sighed, studying him, shaking her head. "Don't you have some hot date tonight with a barista or something?"

"Nah... Figured I'd try and help my partner out... you know. Like a good cop."

"You're a fed now. Not a cop."

"Right... well, it's what my dad woulda done," he said, shrugging nonchalantly. But now, as she calmed, she realized this was an olive branch. He'd gone out of his way for her. Out of genuine concern.

Tom wasn't a nosy sort. He wasn't a gossip monger. He truly cared for his partners...

And now... she wasn't sure how uncomfortable she was allowed to be.

She tried to bite back her discomfort, and any scathing reply. Instead, she said, "Th-thanks..."

"Sure!" he brightened.

She reached out, patting him on the arm.

"Are you gonna read it?"

She considered it, but decided that would be *too* much vulnerability.

"Soon. After I finish my run. Er... thanks Tom."

"Yeah... umm... yeah... Well. I guess I should be going." He hesitated as if wanting her to say something, but then he shrugged and turned. As he walked away, she paused. Frowned. She pictured that waitress' phone number, and how she'd felt when she'd seen it.

"Hey, Tom!" she called.

He turned sharply.

"Why don't we get a bite. My treat this time."

He looked at her, eyebrows up. "Y-yeah... sure. Sure sound great." He wrinkled his nose. "Not Chinese again, though. Right?"

"Hell yeah. Always Chinese."

He chuckled, but shrugged. "Fine... Whatever. Your call, if you're paying."

She forced a smile and a nod, but her hand hovered near her pocket, touching against the piece of paper. The folded letter.

She'd read it later.

A letter from her parents? Lost in evidence for a decade?

She felt a flicker of excitement course down her spine, and then she turned, moving towards where her partner waited in the door leading out of the track.

NOW AVAILABLE!

IN THE EYES
(An Elle Keen Suspense Thriller—Book 3)

As murders mimicking historical assassinations plague the city, only FBI Agent Elle Keen can decipher the deadly puzzle before history repeats itself once more…

"The plot has many twists and turns, but it is the ending, which I did not see coming at all, that totally defines this book as one of the most riveting that I have read in years."
—Reader review for Not Like Us

IN THE EYES is book #3 in a long-anticipated new series by #1 bestseller Ava Strong, whose bestseller NOT LIKE US (a free download) has received over 1,000 five star ratings and reviews. The series begins with IN THE DARK (book #1).

An enthralling crime thriller with a captivating and complex female protagonist, Elle Keen is a riveting mystery series with non-stop action, suspense, and unexpected plot twists that are guaranteed to keep you on the edge of your seat well into the night. Fans of Robert Dugoni, Karin Slaughter, and Lisa Gardner are sure to fall in love.

Future books in the series are also available.

"This is a chilling, suspenseful page turner that just might leave you scared at night!"
—Reader review for Not Like Us

"Very intriguing, kept me turning page after page… Lots of twists and turns and a very unexpected ending. Cannot wait for the next in this series!"
—Reader review for Not Like Us

"A roller coaster ride of events… Can't put down until you finish it!"

—Reader review for Not Like Us

"Excellent read with very realistic characters that you become emotionally invested in… Couldn't put it down!"
—Reader review for The Death Code

"An excellent read, lots of twists and turns, with a surprising ending, leaving you wanting to read the next book in the series! Well done!"
—Reader review for The Death Code

"Well worth the read. Cannot wait to see what happens in the next book!"
—Reader review for The Death Code

"Quickly became a story I couldn't put down! I highly recommend this book!"
—Reader review for His Other Wife

"I really enjoyed the fast-paced action, plot design and characterization... I didn't want to put the book down and the ending was a total surprise."
—Reader review for His Other Wife

"The characters are extremely well developed… There are twists and turns in the plot that kept me guessing. An extremely well written story."
—Reader review for His Other Wife

"One of the best books I have ever read… The ending was perfect and surprising. Ava Strong is an amazing writer."
—Reader review for His Other Wife

"Holy cow, what a rollercoaster… Many times I absolutely KNEW who the killer was—only to be proven wrong each time. I was completely surprised by the ending. I have to say, I am thrilled that this is the first in a series. My only complaint is that the next one isn't out yet. I need it!"
—Reader review for His Other Wife

"An incredible, intense, spellbinding, enjoyable story. It will keep you captivated until the end."

—Reader review for His Other Wife

Ava Strong

Ava Strong is author of the REMI LAURENT mystery series, comprising six books (and counting); of the ILSE BECK mystery series, comprising seven books (and counting); of the STELLA FALL psychological suspense thriller series, comprising six books (and counting); of the DAKOTA STEELE FBI suspense thriller series, comprising six books (and counting); of the LILY DAWN suspense thriller series, comprising five books (and counting); the MEGAN YORK FBI suspense thriller series, comprising five books (and counting); the SOFIA BLAKE FBI suspense thriller series, comprising five books (and counting); the AMY RUSH FBI suspense thriller series, comprising five books (and counting); the ELLE KEEN FBI suspense thriller series, comprising five books (and counting); and the LEXI COLE suspense thriller series, comprising five books (and counting).

An avid reader and lifelong fan of the mystery and thriller genres, Ava loves to hear from you, so please feel free to visit www.avastrongauthor.com to learn more and stay in touch.

BOOKS BY AVA STRONG

ELLE KEEN FBI SUSPENSE THRILLER
IN THE DARK (Book #1)
IN THE WAY (Book #2)
IN THE EYES (Book #3)
IN THE NIGHT (Book #4)
IN THE SILENCE (Book #5)

AMY RUSH FBI SUSPENSE THRILLER
TWISTED TRUTH (Book #1)
TWISTED GAME (Book #2)
TWISTED SECRET (Book #3)
TWISTED FATE (Book #4)
TWISTED VOW (Book #5)

SOFIA BLAKE FBI SUSPSENSE THRILLER
NO ONE THERE (Book #1)
NO ONE LEFT (Book #2)
NO ONE HOME (Book #3)
NO ONE TO HELP (Book #4)
NO ONE LIKE THIS (Book #5)

MEGAN YORK FBI SUSPENSE THRILLER
YOU'LL BE SORRY (Book #1)
YOU'LL BE NEXT (Book #2)
YOU'LL BE MINE (Book #3)
YOU'LL BE FIRST (Book #4)
YOU'LL BE GONE (Book #5)

LILY DAWN FBI SUSPENSE THRILLER
STILL ALIVE (Book #1)
STILL HOPE (Book #2)
STILL AWAKE (Book #3)
STILL HERE (Book #4)
STILL MAD (Book #5)

REMI LAURENT FBI SUSPENSE THRILLER
THE DEATH CODE (Book #1)
THE MURDER CODE (Book #2)
THE MALICE CODE (Book #3)
THE VENGEANCE CODE (Book #4)
THE DECEPTION CODE (Book #5)
THE SEDUCTION CODE (Book #6)

ILSE BECK FBI SUSPENSE THRILLER
NOT LIKE US (Book #1)
NOT LIKE HE SEEMED (Book #2)
NOT LIKE YESTERDAY (Book #3)
NOT LIKE THIS (Book #4)
NOT LIKE SHE THOUGHT (Book #5)
NOT LIKE BEFORE (Book #6)
NOT LIKE NORMAL (Book #7)

STELLA FALL PSYCHOLOGICAL SUSPENSE THRILLER
HIS OTHER WIFE (Book #1)
HIS OTHER LIE (Book #2)
HIS OTHER SECRET (Book #3)
HIS OTHER MISTRESS (Book #4)
HIS OTHER LIFE (Book #5)
HIS OTHER TRUTH (Book #6)

DAKOTA STEELE FBI SUSPENSE THRILLER
WITHOUT MERCY (Book #1)
WITHOUT REMORSE (Book #2)
WITHOUT A PAST (Book #3)
WITHOUT PITY (Book #4)
WITHOUT HOPE (Book #5)

LEXI COLE SUSPENSE THRILLER
FEAR THE DARK (Book #1)
FEAR THE SILENCE (Book #2)
FEAR THE COLD (Book #3)
FEAR THE NIGHT (Book #4)
FEAR THE TRUTH (Book #5)

Printed in Great Britain
by Amazon

44920812R00091